The Loner:
SEVEN DAYS TO DIE

The Loner:
SEVEN DAYS TO DIE

J. A. Johnstone

PINNACLE BOOKS
Kensington Publishing Corp.

www.kensingtonbooks.com

PINNACLE BOOKS are published by

Kensington Publishing Corp.
119 West 40th Street
New York, NY 10018

All Kensington titles, imprints, and distributed lines are
available at special quantity discounts for bulk purchases
for sales promotions, premiums, fund-raising, educational,
or institutional use. Special book excerpts or customized
printings can also be created to fit specific needs. For details,
write or phone the office of the Kensington special sales
manager: Kensington Publishing Corp., 119 West 40th
Street, New York, NY 10018, attn: Special Sales Department;
phone 1-800-221-2647.

PINNACLE BOOKS and the Pinnacle logo are Reg. U.S.
Pat. & TM Off.

ISBN-13: 978-0-7860-2279-3
ISBN-10: 0-7860-2279-5

First printing: July 2010

10 9 8 7 6 5 4 3 2 1

Printed in the United States of America

Chapter 1

Somewhere not far off, a wolf howled in the night.

The lonely sound brought a hint of a smile to the face of the man who had once been Conrad Browning. He leaned forward to stir the little fire where his coffeepot bubbled, careful not to look directly into the flames as he did so. That could ruin a man's night vision.

Not being able to see well if danger threatened could ruin a man's life. It could end it, in fact.

The man who was now Kid Morgan settled back on the flat rock he was using as a seat and listened to the wolf sing its solitary song. He felt a bond of kinship with the beast. The wolf was probably a loner, too—at least The Kid liked to think that was the case.

But maybe it wasn't true. Maybe the wolf had a mate.

The Kid's mouth tightened into a thin line. He shook his head. Couldn't be. The long, ululating wails directed at the night sky had such a mournful sound to them he knew the creature must have experienced pain and loss.

Like him.

"Stop feeling sorry for yourself," he said aloud as he reached for the coffeepot, using a piece of leather to protect his hand as he grasped its handle.

He wasn't sure if he was talking to himself or the wolf.

"It's been a year," he whispered as he poured coffee into his cup. "A year."

In some ways it seemed much longer than that, in others only the blink of an eye since he'd been a happily married, successful businessman with a beautiful wife he adored.

Now he was a wanderer, a man with no home and a new name, not the one he'd been born with. Tragically, his wife had died at the hands of evil men. Conrad Browning had died in the crucible of that tragedy, and from the ashes had risen Kid Morgan, the gunfighter. The avenger. The man who rode alone.

In the months since then, he had settled the score with the people responsible for Rebel's death, and although he had drawn no satisfaction from his actions, the knowledge that justice had been done had eased some of his nightmares.

It was bleak comfort, but better than nothing.

Once that grim chore was done, The Kid had wanted only to be left alone, but trouble kept drawing him in. There were people who needed help, and he hadn't been able to turn his back on them.

Once he would have, without a second thought, but after being married to Rebel and forming a friendship with his long-estranged father, Frank Morgan, he no longer possessed the smug, self-righteous callousness that had plagued him while he was growing up. Despite his desire for solitude, when he saw innocent people being threatened or taken advantage of, he had to take a hand.

In those moments, he knew what it was like to make contact with another human being again. In recent weeks, he had wanted to put away the grief for a while, to reach out and smile and laugh and be happy, even if only for a few minutes.

He couldn't allow that. When somebody died, people talked about a suitable period of mourning. Well, for him a suitable period was the rest of his life. Out of respect for what he'd lost, the grief could never go away.

That's why he was sitting in that isolated camp in the rugged mountains of New Mexico Territory. As far as he knew, he was the only human being within a dozen miles or more . . . and that was just the way he wanted it.

He sipped his coffee. He'd already eaten a scanty meal of biscuits and jerky. His plan was to nurse the cup of coffee for a little while before turning in.

His buckskin gelding, which had been grazing a few yards away, suddenly lifted its head and made a soft nickering sound. The horse's ears pricked forward.

He noticed it, as he would anything else that might be a sign of danger. Moving with the smooth, efficient grace of a panther, he stood and set the cup on the rock. He reached down and picked up his Winchester from the ground where he'd placed it next to the bedroll he had already spread out.

With a bare whisper of noise, he slid into the brush, leaving the tiny fire crackling behind him.

The buckskin whinnied louder, scenting another horse. Fine, thought The Kid. If somebody was out there in the darkness, he wanted to draw them in, making them easier to deal with.

He wore a black hat, black coat, black trousers and boots, helping him blend into the shadows. He waited patiently.

Time stretched out, but time didn't have much meaning for him anymore. He didn't have anywhere he had to be at any particular time. He didn't have anywhere he had to be, period. No one he knew would be looking for him.

Conrad Browning's lawyers were aware that he was alive, but they didn't know where he was. They ran the businesses and banked the profits, and that was the way it would be for the foreseeable future.

Frank Morgan knew, too, but Frank was even more of a drifter than his son. People even called him The Drifter, in fact. He was one of the last truly fast guns. He was off somewhere, doing whatever it was he did. He had made it clear, the last time he and The Kid saw each other, that he would respect his son's desire for privacy.

So whoever was skulking around, it wasn't a friend of his, The Kid told himself. It might not necessarily be an enemy . . . but he was going to assume the worst until he learned otherwise.

After a few more minutes, he heard the thud of a horse's hoof against the earth. A moment later, brush rustled. Then a man's voice spoke. The Kid couldn't make out the words, but he understood some of the reply from a second man.

". . . around here somewhere, I tell you. I caught a glimpse of his fire."

So there was more than one of them. And they *were* looking for him. They had tracked him by his campfire.

He had considered making a cold camp, but he didn't think it was necessary. He had believed he was alone on the mountainside.

Obviously, that had been a mistake.

"Spread out." That was a third voice. "Lewis, over there. Hargrove, take the left flank. Murphy, go right. Kinnard and I will take the middle."

So there were at least five men searching for him. Or rather, searching for *somebody,* The Kid corrected. He didn't think they had reason to be after *him,* but he'd been mixed up in enough trouble over the past year he was bound to have left some enemies behind him.

Maybe he ought to confront them, demand to know who they were looking for. If it came to a fight, five-to-one odds were pretty steep, but he had faced worse.

A cold smile tugged at his mouth as the searchers came closer, making their way up the slope. They were making quite a bit of noise. The buckskin had given The Kid some advance warning, but even if that hadn't happened, he would have heard the men long before they reached his camp.

He could see the fire from where he crouched in the brush. The flames had died down to embers, but they still glowed redly. The scent of wood smoke hung in the air along with the smell of Arbuckle's coffee. It was enough to lead one of the men right to the camp.

"I found it," the man called eagerly.

A moment later, The Kid's keen eyes vaguely made out the dark shapes of the others as they converged on the clearing and stepped out into the open.

"He was here," one of the men said excitedly.

"He's still here somewhere," said another. "His horse is unsaddled and hobbled right over there. He can't be far off. We'll spread out and look for him."

"Hey, where'd Haggarty go?" one of the men asked.

"Who gives a damn about Haggarty? If he

wandered off, that means there'll be one less of us with a claim on that reward money, don't it?"

. "Yeah, you're right, Deke. I hadn't thought about it like that."

Reward? What was going on? There was no reward on The Kid's head, at least not as far as he knew. He had broken plenty of laws . . . in fact, he had killed men in cold blood . . . but he had never been charged with anything.

Those manhunters had the wrong man.

Maybe he ought to step out and tell them that, he thought. But would they believe him? Or would they just start shooting and ask questions later?

He decided to lie low and wait them out. If they spread out like their leader had said, he might be able to jump them one at a time and put them out of action. He didn't want to kill anybody unless he had to, but he would defend himself.

Once again the man in charge—Deke, that was his name—separated the others. They moved off, heading up the heavily forested hillside.

One of them moved straight toward the spot where The Kid waited in the brush.

Chapter 2

With infinite patience, The Kid remained motionless. The searcher was going to pass just to his right. Silently, he lifted the Winchester, waited until the man stepped past him, and slammed the rifle butt against the back of the man's neck.

You could kill somebody like that if you hit them hard enough, but The Kid eased off so the blow wasn't fatal. The man dropped like a rock, out cold. He'd never had a chance to cry out.

He hadn't made much noise falling down, but it was enough to alert one of the other men. He turned and bounded through the brush toward The Kid, calling softly, "Hargrove, you all right?"

There was no time to do anything except confront the man. The Kid used the Winchester again, whipping the stock around so it smashed across the man's jaw. He went down, groaning as he fell.

"Over there!" Deke yelled. "Hargrove and Murphy must have cornered him!"

Things were about to get worse. But at least The Kid had whittled down the odds a little.

A crashing in the brush made him wheel to his left. As he did so, Colt flame blossomed like a crimson flower in the night, and he heard a solid *thunk!* as a slug struck a tree trunk near him.

"Don't kill him!" Deke again shouted orders. "They want him alive!"

They? Who were *they?*

The Kid didn't have time to ponder that, as one of the men charged him. He went low, thrust out a booted foot, and his leg swept the man's legs out from under him. With a startled yell, the man plunged headfirst into a pine tree. The Kid winced at the sound of skull hitting bark.

The man didn't get up, didn't even move.

"Hargrove! Murphy! Lewis! Answer me, damn it!"

"Deke, I don't like this. You know what he's like. He might've killed all of them by now."

"Shut up! There's five of us and only one of him."

"There *was* five of us. You heard. They didn't answer."

A bitter curse came from Deke. The two men were to The Kid's right. He circled behind them as they cast back and forth, looking for their companions and the man they were hunting.

It was pathetic, thought The Kid. They weren't professional manhunters, that was for sure. Probably cowboys whose heads had been filled up with the thought of getting their hands on some reward money.

He didn't want to hurt them, but he knew they were dangerous. They would spook easily and start shooting again, and a bullet didn't care who pulled the trigger. They might actually spray enough lead around to hit him by accident.

He moved up in the shadows behind one of the men and drew his Colt. Pressing the revolver's barrel against a suddenly stiffening back, he ordered in a low, harsh voice, "Don't move, mister, or I'll blow your spine in two."

The Kid heard a sharp intake of breath. "Oh, my God," the man said. "Deke! He's got me, Deke!"

The Kid shoved the gun harder into the man's back. "I didn't tell you to yell, Kinnard." He plucked the man's name out of his memory.

"You . . . you know who I am?"

"Yeah. And if you don't get the hell off this mountain and take your friends with you, I'll show up some night when you don't know I'm anywhere around. You know what'll happen then, don't you, Kinnard?"

The Kid made his voice as rough and threatening as he could. At the same time, he had to make an effort not to laugh. Grim and dangerous though it was, it was a game of sorts, a game he was about to win.

"Drop your guns," he went on. "I want to hear them hit the ground." Then he raised his voice. "Deke! You better come up here where I can see you, Deke, or I'll kill your partner."

For a moment there was no response. Then The Kid heard a defeated sigh.

"Take it easy. There's no need for anybody to die."

"Then why'd you come up here hunting me?" The Kid ground the gun barrel into Kinnard's back, drawing a yelp of pain from him. "Drop your guns, I said. You, too, Deke. Step out where I can see you and get those guns on the ground."

"You got to do what he says, Deke," Kinnard pleaded. "He knows who we are, damn it!"

With a rustling of brush, Deke stepped into the open. He put his rifle on the ground, drew a revolver from a holster at his waist and dropped it as well. Kinnard threw his rifle down and fumbled his gun from its holster. It thudded to the ground.

"That's it," Deke said. "We're disarmed."

"No hide-out guns?"

"No. I swear."

The Kid didn't believe him, but it didn't really matter. He said, "Deke, sit down next to that tree. Kinnard, take your belt off and use it to tie him to the trunk."

"What . . . what're you gonna do to me?" Kinnard asked.

"I'll kill you if you don't do what I tell you."

Cursing, Deke sat down where The Kid ordered. Kinnard lashed him securely to the narrow trunk of a fairly small pine. When that was done, Kinnard asked nervously, "What about me?"

"Turn around," The Kid said.

Kinnard started to blubber. "Oh, God. Oh, no, mister, please don't kill me. Please. You can't—"

The Kid flipped the Colt around and shut him up with a quick rap from the gun butt. Kinnard's knees unhinged and dumped him on the ground at Deke's feet.

"Your other three men are scattered along the slope here, knocked out," The Kid told Deke. "One of them hit his head pretty hard against a tree. I hope he's not hurt too bad."

Deke glared up at him. "You made the worst mistake of your life, Bledsoe."

"I sort of doubt that," The Kid said. "And I'm not—"

The crash of a gunshot interrupted him. What felt like a giant fist smashed into his body and drove him forward. He ran into a tree and bounced off. His balance deserted him. He felt himself falling and couldn't stop it.

The Kid smacked face-first into the ground. Pain filled him and made his head spin crazily. He heard footsteps approaching him. Forcing his eyes open, he saw a pair of booted feet stop right beside him. The man bent over him and said in an icy voice, "Yeah, you made a mistake, all right, you just didn't know it. You turned your back on me."

"Haggarty!" Deke cried. "Haggarty, you got him! Let me loose, and we'll get the others and take him in."

Haggarty laughed. "And split the reward six ways when I earned it by myself? The hell with that."

"You can't collect if he's dead."

"He's not dead. I just creased him. He's stunned now, but he'll live."

"You gotta let me loose, anyway," Deke persisted. "You can't just leave us all up here like this!"

Haggarty grunted. "Get yourself loose. I don't have time for you."

A hand grasped The Kid's shoulder, rolled him onto his back. A fresh burst of agony shot through him.

"I've been watching," the dark, looming shape that was Haggarty said. "I knew you were a dangerous man, Bledsoe, but I wasn't sure you could take all five of them like you did. Once I saw that, I knew I couldn't give you a chance."

The Kid forced his tongue out of his mouth and licked his lips. He husked, "I . . . I'm not . . ."

Before he could get the words out, he saw a gun butt whipping down toward his head.

The night exploded in a burst of shooting stars, and that was the last thing The Kid knew.

Chapter 3

Bledsoe.

Who the hell was Bledsoe?

The question echoed in The Kid's brain as consciousness slowly seeped back into it. Then pain overwhelmed curiosity and he forgot all about Bledsoe. Instead, he fought not to be sick as nausea roiled his stomach.

He felt a horrible pounding inside his skull and realized he was hanging head down. That torture was his pulse, he figured out after a moment. It felt like imps from hell banging on the inside of his head with ball-peen hammers.

The fire in his side was bad. It hurt like someone had jammed a blazing torch into his body. Maybe they had.

The swaying and bouncing added to his sickness. He tried to move, hoping to find a more comfortable position. His hands were numb, which meant his wrists were tied together. Eventually, he came to understand that his wrists were also bound to his ankles.

Somebody had draped him facedown over a saddle and lashed him in place so he couldn't move.

Haggarty.

That son of a bitch.

The Kid couldn't hold back the groan of misery that welled up in his throat. A couple of seconds after the wretched sound escaped, the horse that was carrying him stopped.

"So, you're awake again," a man's voice said.

"Cut me . . . loose," The Kid gasped.

"Yeah, like I'm gonna take a chance on cutting Bloody Ben Bledsoe loose."

"Hag . . . Haggarty?"

"That's right."

The Kid was too weak to lift his head to look at the man. He stared at the ground as he said, "You've got the wrong man, you stupid bastard."

Haggarty chuckled. "Talk like that's not likely to make me want to treat you better, is it? I've seen the picture on all the reward posters. You're Bledsoe, all right."

"You're wrong. My name is . . . Morgan."

During that brief hesitation, he had thought about saying Conrad Browning. But that name probably wouldn't mean anything to Haggarty. At one point, Conrad had been declared legally dead, after a body was found in the charred ruins of his house in Carson City. Later, Conrad's lawyers had discreetly informed the authorities that he was, in fact, still alive, but his whereabouts were unknown.

That was the way The Kid wanted to keep it. He had no interest in going back to his previous life, and he didn't want to reveal it unless he had to.

"You can lie all you want to, Bledsoe," Haggarty went on. "No one is going to believe you. Who'd take the word of a murdering outlaw?"

With a click of his tongue, Haggarty got the horses moving again. As The Kid swayed over the saddle and a fresh wave of dizziness set the world to spinning crazily around him, he realized he was just going to have to bide his time.

Surely, sooner or later, Haggarty would deliver him to someone who would realize a terrible mistake had been made.

The Kid could tell from the light it was early morning. He had been out cold for most of the night. The light grew brighter and the shadows shorter as the sun climbed in the New Mexico sky. The ride seemed to take an eternity.

Finally, Haggarty reined in again. "There it is," he said. "Hell Gate. You're back home, Bledsoe."

The Kid forced his head up and gazed out across a valley. On the far side, backed up against a sheer cliff of what appeared to be solid granite, was a compound of squat stone buildings, surrounded by a high, thick, stone wall with guard towers at the front corners. The cliff itself formed the rear wall of the enclosure.

In the middle of the cliff was a tunnel opening that reminded The Kid of the black, hungry maw of a beast. The resemblance was made even stronger by a pair of heavy, barred gates that looked like teeth.

One thought blazed through The Kid's mind as he stared at the compound. *Once a man was swallowed up by that hole, he would never come out again.* "What . . . what is that place?" he muttered.

"Hell Gate Territorial Prison," Haggarty said. "You know that as well as I do, Bledsoe. It's where they put the worst of the worst . . . like you."

The Kid didn't have the energy to argue with his captor. Actually, he felt somewhat relieved as he lowered his head again. Now that they had reached their destination, somebody at Hell Gate Prison was bound to realize he wasn't Bloody Ben Bledsoe, whoever that was.

He supposed maybe Haggarty had made an honest mistake in thinking he was an outlaw who had escaped from the prison.

It didn't change the fact that once The Kid was back on his feet again, he would have a score to settle with the man. Mistake or not, Haggarty would pay for what he had done. Nobody gunned down Kid Morgan from behind, pistol-whipped him, and got away with it.

Haggarty hitched the horses into motion again, leading The Kid's buckskin with The Kid lashed to the saddle. Though the prison had appeared close in the thin, clear mountain air, they had to travel several miles on horseback to get there. It took a long time to wind down the trail into the valley, cross it, and climb the other side.

At last they came to a pair of massive wooden gates in the stone wall. Guard towers sat on both sides of the entrance. The Kid couldn't tilt his head back far enough to see the occupants of the towers, but he heard a harsh voice call down, "Is that Bledsoe?"

"That's right," Haggarty replied.

The Kid didn't waste time and strength contradicting him. Presenting the facts to a guard wouldn't do any good. He needed to talk to the warden.

With a creaking of hinges, one of the gates was soon swung open. Haggarty rode in, leading The Kid's buckskin. Blue-uniformed guards clustered around them, carrying rifles.

One of the men thumbed back his black cap and nodded. "It's Bledsoe, all right," he declared. "I'd recognize that face anywhere. Pure evil, it is."

Haggarty dismounted. The Kid saw his booted feet and denim-clad legs approaching. Haggarty leaned over, and for the first time The Kid saw his face, heavy-jawed and hard-planed, with several days' worth of dark stubble on his cheeks.

Haggarty grinned coldly at him. "Don't try anything, Bledsoe," he warned. "There are a dozen guards surrounding you, and they'd like nothing better than an excuse to settle the score for the two men you killed when you broke out of here."

The Kid didn't say anything. He waited and felt

a tug on his wrists and ankles as Haggarty used a knife to cut the rope that bound them together.

He might have fallen headfirst to the ground and broken his neck, but Haggarty caught hold of the back of his shirt and hauled him the other way, so that he slid out of the saddle onto his feet.

As soon as he landed, his balance deserted him. After hanging upside down for so long, earth and sky had traded places for him. As they abruptly switched back into their proper orientation, The Kid fell, sitting down hard in the dust. His stomach spasmed, and he couldn't hold the sickness back any longer. He crumpled onto his side and painfully emptied his belly.

As the retching subsided, he became aware that the men surrounding him were laughing. He wanted to curse them bitterly but knew it wouldn't do any good.

Haggarty was the one who really had some payback coming. The Kid intended to deliver it just as soon as he possibly could.

Chapter 4

Haggarty wore a long duster and a brown hat. He was big, broad across the shoulders, and deep in the chest. He stood a couple inches over six feet, which made him slightly taller than The Kid. He probably outweighed The Kid by fifty pounds.

Haggarty reached down, lifted him effortlessly, and had no trouble manhandling him toward one of the stone buildings. The Kid's wrists were still tied, but his feet were free. Haggarty had cut the bonds around his ankles.

Waving lazily in the breeze, the flags of the United States and New Mexico Territory flew on a flagpole in front of the building that was their destination. The Kid figured it was the prison's administration building.

Blue-uniformed men went in and out of a larger structure to the right. That would be the guards' barracks, The Kid thought.

He took his mind off how horrible he felt by

studying the rest of the layout, now that he was on his feet again and could look around.

Smoke rising from the chimney of a building to the left made him think it was probably the kitchen and mess hall. Several smaller buildings clustered around it. One of them would be the armory, where the guards' rifles and ammunition were kept. Another appeared to be a blacksmith shop. The rest were probably for storage of various sorts.

Two more buildings that looked like barracks stood near the towering cliff. The windows in them had iron bars, and barbed-wire fence was strung between posts driven into the ground around them. Armed guards paced back and forth nearby.

Clearly, some of the prison's inmates were kept in those buildings. If that was true, where did the barred tunnel in the cliff face lead?

The Kid suspected he knew the answer, and it wasn't a pretty one.

Trailed by the guards who had laughed at his misery, The Kid and Haggarty reached the steps that led up to the administration building's porch.

"Are you through being sick?" Haggarty asked. "I don't want you throwing up on the warden's boots. He's still got to approve paying me the reward."

The Kid swallowed the foul taste in his mouth and rasped, "I'm all right."

That wasn't exactly true. He felt weak as a

kitten. His head ached intolerably, his side hurt like blazes, and he was still a little dizzy. But his stomach was settling down the longer he was upright, and he didn't think he would be sick again.

With Haggarty's fingers digging cruelly and painfully into his shoulder, The Kid went up the steps. His boots thudded on the planks as Haggarty gave him a shove that sent him stumbling toward the door. A guard opened it before The Kid could crash into it.

He tripped as he entered the building and fell to his knees. Haggarty grabbed his arm and lifted him again. They were in an office with several desks. Men in suits who worked at those desks stood and stared at him.

Another man waited in an open doorway on the other side of the room. He was tall and slender and wore a sober black suit and a string tie. Wavy dark hair receded from a high forehead. The man's face was like a wedge angling back from a prominent nose. A neatly trimmed mustache adorned his upper lip. His eyes were large and had an odd cast to them. He clasped his hands together behind his back and rocked back and forth on his toes.

"Haggarty," he said. "They told me you were bringing in Bledsoe. I didn't believe it. I didn't think one man would be able to capture such a monster."

The Kid waited for the man to go on. He waited to hear *This isn't Bledsoe! What the hell were you thinking, Haggarty?*

Instead, the man rocked back and forth, smiled, and said, "Bring him in. I'm looking forward to telling him what he has in store for him now that he's back at Hell Gate."

"No!" The Kid cried, unable to hold in the startled exclamation. "Can't you see I'm not this fellow Bledsoe, whoever he is?"

Haggarty chuckled. "He's been saying that ever since I nabbed him last night, Warden Fletcher."

"Well, we'll soon make him understand that he's not fooling anybody." Fletcher gave Haggarty a curt nod and stepped back into what was obviously the warden's private office.

Haggarty shoved The Kid forward into the room. It was well-appointed, with a big desk, several leather armchairs, a map of New Mexico Territory on one wall and portraits of the president and the territorial governor on the opposite wall. Behind the desk, a window looked out over the compound and the tunnel that had been bored into the cliff.

Haggarty dragged a ladderback chair from one side of the room and put it directly in front of the desk. A heavy hand on The Kid's shoulder forced him down into the chair. The Kid sat there while Fletcher went behind the desk and regarded him coolly.

"I'll wire Santa Fe that you've been recaptured, Bledsoe," he said. "I'm sure that will be welcome news."

The Kid hadn't noticed telegraph wires coming

into the prison, but he hadn't been in a very good position to look around much.

He shook his head stubbornly. "You're making a mistake. My name's not Bledsoe. I'm not an escaped prisoner. I've never been here before."

Fletcher had been about to sit down, but he stopped himself and straightened as The Kid spoke. He murmured, "Is that so?" and came around the desk again to stand in front of The Kid.

With no warning, his fist lashed out. It crashed into The Kid's jaw with terrific force and knocked him out of the chair. Fletcher might be slender, but he packed a lot of force in his punch. The Kid sprawled on the floor.

"Pick him up," Fletcher snapped at Haggarty.

Once The Kid was back in the chair, still stunned but able to sit up by himself, Fletcher went on, "I see dried blood on his head and on his shirt. What happened to him?"

"Had to shoot him," Haggarty replied. "I was careful just to crease him in the side. It knocked him down, made him lose some blood. I figured he wouldn't feel much like fighting after that, but I gave him a rap on the head with my gun butt, just to be sure."

"He's not badly hurt?"

Haggarty shook his head. "No, I cleaned the wound and bandaged it. I can't rule out blood poisoning, but I'm pretty sure he'll live."

"We'll have the doctor look him over just to be sure. I'd hate to have him die before he can be hanged."

"No offense, Warden, but I don't think a jury's going to sentence Bledsoe to be hanged."

"He killed two of my guards," Fletcher said with a frown.

"I know. But he's also the only one who knows where he stashed all that money he and his gang stole."

The words cut through the ringing in The Kid's head. He remembered how, a couple of years earlier, his father Frank had helped recover some money that had been looted from a bank that was part of the Browning business interests. He'd been locked up in Yuma Prison, over in Arizona, for a while.

In that case, several people on the outside had known Frank's true identity. Kid's case was different. Those idiots actually *believed* he was some outlaw named Bledsoe.

"I think the murder of two prison guards takes precedence over a bank robbery," Fletcher said, irritation evident in his voice.

"I think so, too, Warden," Haggarty said, "but the men who own those banks have a lot of influence in Santa Fe. That's all I'm saying."

"Well, I hope you're wrong. I'd like to see justice done." Fletcher took hold of The Kid's sandy hair and jerked his head back. "Why don't you just tell us where that money is, Bledsoe, and save us all a great deal of trouble?"

The Kid bit back the curse that wanted to spring from his lips. Angering Fletcher wouldn't do any good. Instead he forced himself to say in a calm voice, "Warden, listen to me. *I'm not Bledsoe.* I didn't kill any of your men, and I don't know anything about any bank loot."

Haggarty laughed. "You're trying that lie on the wrong man, mister. If there's anybody who knows that you're really Bloody Ben Bledsoe, it's Jonas Fletcher."

"That's right," Fletcher said with a nod. "I'm not likely to forget you, Bledsoe. Not after all the trouble you caused, even before your escape. You didn't really think that shaving off your beard would make you that difficult to recognize, did you?"

It was insane, thought The Kid. Haggarty was going by pictures on wanted posters, which were sometimes notoriously inaccurate, and Fletcher seemed to be so full of anger and hate that he wanted to believe the man who'd escaped from his prison and killed two guards had been recaptured.

Fletcher had some reason for lying about it. The Kid couldn't begin to figure out what that might be.

"How about it?" Fletcher prodded. "Things might go a little easier for you if you cooperate."

"I can't tell you what I don't know," The Kid replied between clenched teeth. "I'm not Bledsoe."

Fletcher stared at him for a long moment before saying, "All right, suit yourself. You may change your mind after a spell in Hades." He looked up at Haggarty. "We'll take charge of him now. Your job is done."

"The laborer is worthy of his hire. Isn't that what the Good Book says, Warden? I've heard that you used to be a preacher."

"Don't quote Scripture to me," Fletcher snapped. "That was a long time ago. Don't worry, Haggarty. When I wire Santa Fe, I'll include the fact that it was you who brought him back to us. You'll have to ride to Santa Fe to collect the reward, though."

Haggarty's broad shoulders rose and fell in a shrug. "I don't care where I have to go, as long as I get paid." He paused. "You think maybe I could get something to eat before I leave, maybe some grain and water for my horse?"

Fletcher nodded and called, "Dawkins."

One of the men from the outer office stuck his head in the door. "Yes, Warden?"

"See to it that Mr. Haggarty gets whatever he needs for himself and his mount," Fletcher ordered.

"Yes, sir."

Haggarty asked, "What about the horse Bledsoe was riding? I brought him in on it."

Fletcher waved a hand. "You can have it as far as I'm concerned. Count it as a bonus on the reward."

"I'll do that," Haggarty said with a nod. "That buckskin looks like a fine piece of horseflesh."

The Kid wouldn't have thought it possible under the circumstances, but his heart sank a little more. He and the buckskin had been through a lot together over the past year. He hated to lose the horse, especially to a brutal son of a bitch like Haggarty.

But of course, he had more important things to worry about.

Like the fact that he was about to be tossed into someplace called Hades. He knew Fletcher must have been talking about the dark tunnel into the cliff. A place known as Hades, in a prison called Hell Gate . . .

That couldn't be good.

Chapter 5

Haggarty left the office, and two of the rifle-toting guards stepped in to keep an eye on The Kid. Fletcher went behind his desk and sat down. He pulled a piece of paper in front of him and dipped a pen in an inkwell.

"While we're waiting for the doctor, I'll compose the wire that I'll be sending to Santa Fe," he said.

"How about sending a wire for me?" The Kid asked.

Fletcher's eyes narrowed. "Who in God's name to?"

"My lawyers in San Francisco. Claudius Turnbuckle and John Stafford. Maybe you've heard of them."

The warden's eyebrows went up instead of down. "As a matter of fact, I *haven't* heard of them, but I find it hard to believe that a bloody-handed outlaw like you would have lawyers in San Francisco, Bledsoe."

"That's because I'm not Bledsoe." Before

Fletcher could lose his temper and hit him again, The Kid played the closest thing he had to a trump card. "My name is Conrad Browning. I'm a businessman."

Or at least I was, before my wife was murdered.

Fletcher stared at him for a long moment. The warden's thin lips curved in a smile, and surprisingly, he began to laugh.

"A businessman?" he repeated.

"Surely you've heard of the New Mexico, Rio Grande, and Oriental Railroad Line. It runs from Lordsburg up to a mining town called Ophir." The Kid paused. "I own it."

"You own a railroad?" Fletcher sounded like he was about to laugh again.

"I own stock in *several* railroads. Also silver mines, banks, freight companies, a steamship line—"

Fletcher silenced him with the slash of a hand over the desk. "That's enough. Do you really think I'm crazy enough to believe such claims? What would some sort of . . . some sort of business tycoon be doing wandering around such a godforsaken place as these mountains?"

Because I turned my back on that life when Rebel died, The Kid thought. *Because all I had left to live for was vengeance, and in the end, that wasn't enough. Not nearly enough.*

But Fletcher would neither believe nor understand that, he sensed, so he said, "I was just trying to get away for a while. I am who I say I am, Warden, and if you'll wire Turnbuckle and

Stafford, I can prove it. I'm sure one of them would even come out here and identify me, if that's necessary."

A short bark of laughter came from the warden. "I've already identified you. When you first came here, you sat across this desk from me and cursed me and spat on me. You told me that you'd see me dead. Do you think I'm going to forget that, Bledsoe?"

The Kid didn't answer the question. He said, "Send the wire . . . unless you're afraid to. Tell them you have a man here who claims to be Conrad Browning." The Kid shrugged. "If I'm lying, what do you have to lose?"

"My time," Fletcher snapped. "And that's something I happen to value." He shook his head. "No. I'm not sending any wires for you, Bledsoe."

The Kid wanted to shout *Stop calling me that!* He knew it wouldn't do any good, so he remained silent.

The office door opened, and a stocky man in late middle age came in. A brush of white hair stuck up from his scalp, and he carried a black bag. He was the doctor.

"Sorry it took me a while to get here, Warden," the man said. "I was down in Hades trying to keep a man from bleeding to death. An altercation among the inmates got out of hand, you know."

"Were you successful, Doctor?" Fletcher asked.

"Unfortunately, no. You'll have to assign some

men to a burial detail." The doctor set his bag on
Fletcher's desk, looked at The Kid, and rubbed
his hands together as he smiled, revealing some
poorly fitting false teeth. "Hopefully we'll have
more luck with you, young man."

The Kid wasn't sure he wanted the doctor to
touch him. The man had the air of a quack
about him.

With two armed guards standing by, and
guards who hated him because they believed he
had killed a couple of their comrades, The Kid
knew he would have to cooperate for the time
being.

"I may have to cut that bloody shirt off you,"
the doctor murmured. "Of course, it doesn't
really matter. You'll soon be getting completely
different clothing, anyway."

The Kid sat stoically while the doctor cut the
shirt off and unwound the makeshift bandages
that had been wrapped tightly around his torso.
When the bandages came off, they revealed a
puckered, raw-looking furrow in the flesh of The
Kid's right side.

"Not too bad, not too bad," the doctor said as
if he were talking to himself. He turned his head
to look at Fletcher. "Who tended to this wound
when it was fresh?"

Fletcher was taking a cigar from his vest
pocket. He bit off the end and spat it out before
answering the question. "Tom Haggarty."

"It appears that he did an adequate job." The

doctor opened his bag. "I'll just clean the wound again and bandage it properly."

Fletcher lit the cigar and smoked while the doctor went about his work, humming softly to himself. While The Kid was still Conrad Browning, he had enjoyed a good cigar. The foul-smelling stogie Fletcher was smoking didn't fit that description.

The Kid didn't allow any expression to show on his face when he felt the sting of the carbolic acid the doctor used to clean the wound. Nor did he react when the man covered the bullet crease with pads of clean gauze and bound them in place with strips of bandage that he pulled so tight The Kid could barely breathe.

After that, the doctor examined the gash on The Kid's head where Haggarty had pistol-whipped him. "That could use a couple of stitches to close it up," he said. "Otherwise it's going to leave a little scar."

Fletcher smirked. "I don't think Bledsoe will be too worried about a scar, Dr. Thurber." He left unsaid the implication that a scar wouldn't matter because the man would soon be dangling from the end of a hangrope.

But everyone in the room understood.

Thurber smiled weakly. "It never hurts for a surgeon to practice his art. With your permission, Warden . . . ?"

Fletcher made a magnanimous gesture.

Thurber cleaned the wound first, then took two stitches to close it with a deft touch that surprised

The Kid. He wouldn't have guessed the doctor was that skillful. Thurber bandaged the injury, winding a single strip of bandage around The Kid's head. Then he took hold of The Kid's chin and moved his head to the side. "Nasty looking bruise starting to come up there on the jaw," he commented.

Fletcher sat forward and clamped his teeth tighter on the cigar. "Don't worry about that," he said around the stogie, not bothering to explain that the bruise came from the punch he had handed out to the prisoner.

Thurber began replacing his supplies in the black bag. "Very well," he said. "My services don't seem to be required here any longer. If you need me, though, Warden, don't hesitate to send for me."

"Of course, Doctor."

The white-haired medico nodded to Fletcher, picked up his bag, and bustled out of the office.

Fletcher stood up and put the cigar in an ashtray on his desk. "All right, there's no use postponing this. On your feet, Bledsoe. You're going back to Hades."

The Kid tried one last time. He looked up at Fletcher and said, "I'm not Bledsoe, I tell you. My name is Conrad Browning. Sometimes I'm called Kid Morgan."

One of the guards standing behind The Kid grunted in surprise.

Fletcher looked at him and snapped, "What is it?"

"I've heard of Kid Morgan, Warden. He's some sort of gunfighter. He was mixed up in a big ruckus over in West Texas a while back."

Fletcher sneered. "That doesn't mean *this* man is Kid Morgan. Look at him, Smithson. Doesn't he look like Ben Bledsoe?"

"Well . . . yes, sir, he does, I guess, except for the fact that he doesn't have a beard. But anybody can shave off a beard."

"Exactly."

"I'm just not sure why a man would claim to be a gunfighter if it wasn't true."

"He's trying to save his life," Fletcher said. "He's grasping at straws. Now get him on his feet."

"Yes, sir."

As the two guards moved in, The Kid said, "Take it easy. There's no need for any more rough stuff." He stood up slowly, keeping his hands in plain sight so they would know he wasn't trying some sort of trick.

"There's a full guard detail outside, as I ordered?" Fletcher asked.

"Yes, sir, Warden," the guard called Smithson replied.

"Good. I want Bledsoe completely surrounded, so no one can get to him. Take him straight to Number One."

"Yes, sir."

The Kid wanted to ask what Number One was, but he had a bad feeling he would find out soon enough.

He looked through the window behind Fletcher's

desk and saw that black hole looming in the cliff face. Once again he had the feeling that anybody who went in there might not ever come out again. His instinct was to rebel. His heart slugged heavily in his chest, and he wanted to fight, to run, to do anything he had to do to keep from being put in that hole.

With an effort, he controlled himself. He knew if he put up a struggle, they would knock him out and drag him in there anyway. Injured, alone, and unarmed, the odds were too high against him. No one could have overcome them.

Not even Frank Morgan.

"Let's go, Bledsoe," Smithson said quietly.

The Kid took a deep breath and turned toward the door.

And stopped short because a young woman stood in the doorway, a surprised expression on her beautiful face.

Chapter 6

"Jillian!" Fletcher exclaimed. "What are you doing here? You know you're not supposed to come to my office."

"I-I'm sorry, Father," she said. "Mother was asking for you, and I thought you'd want to come as soon as possible." She peered more intently at The Kid. "Is this . . . ?"

"Yes, Ben Bledsoe," Fletcher said, his voice sharp with impatience. "He's been recaptured."

The Kid saw a bare sliver of a chance. "That's not true, Miss Fletcher," he said quickly. "I'm not Bledsoe. My name is Conrad Brown—"

A rifle butt slammed into the back of The Kid's neck. The blow was a savage one, struck by the second guard at a sharp gesture from the warden. The Kid caught a glimpse of the horrified surprise etched on the young woman's face as he fell.

"This man is a very dangerous prisoner, Jillian," Fletcher said. "I want you to go back to our quarters immediately. You know you're never supposed to leave them without a guard accompanying you."

"I'm sorry, Father, I just . . ."

Jillian Fletcher's voice faded out as The Kid struggled to remain conscious. He had gone through too much in the past eighteen hours, absorbed too much punishment. His body and brain had been stretched as far as they would go.

He managed to lift his head for one last look at the young woman. Her mouth was moving and he could hear the words, but he could no longer make sense of them.

She was beautiful. Petite and well-shaped, with two wings of glossy auburn hair framing her face. Her deep brown eyes locked with his for a second. "Get him up! Get him out of here!" The order came from Fletcher.

Strong hands grasped The Kid's arms and hauled him upright. Jillian Fletcher stepped back so that the guards could shove The Kid through the doorway. The Kid shook his head, trying to clear away the cobwebs, but it was no use.

He was only half conscious as the guards took him through the outer office and outside the administration building. More armed men closed in around him. The two who had hold of his arms marched him past the fenced-off barracks, straight toward the mouth of the tunnel.

The Kid's senses returned to him a little once he was out in the fresh air. He saw two stone walls about three feet tall and topped with sandbags another foot or so high. They formed circles about ten feet in diameter and were fifty feet or so from the tunnel mouth, set to each side of the opening.

Inside each circle was a Gatling gun manned by two guards and pointed at the tunnel. A shudder went through The Kid as he thought about what it would be like if both of those rapid-firers began pouring thousands of rounds through the opening. Nobody inside the tunnel would survive.

The guards took The Kid between the two Gatling gun emplacements. More blue-uniformed men unlocked the gates and swung one side open a few feet. It took two men to move the massive iron gate, even though it swung smoothly on its hinges.

"Everything locked down inside?" Smithson asked the men who opened the gate.

"Yeah, they're all in their holes," one of the men replied.

Smithson and his companion manhandled The Kid into the tunnel. It was fifty feet wide and twenty feet high, with an arched ceiling. The shaft had been bored out of living rock and was braced with thick timbers and vaulted beams. It ran straight into the mountain for a hundred yards.

Both side walls and the rear wall were lined with heavy wooden doors, each with a small, barred window in it. The Kid didn't try to count the doors, but there must have been a hundred

of them. He knew without being told that behind
each door was a cell, also hewn out of the rock.

In the area of the tunnel closest to the gates
were several long tables with benches built onto
them. It was where the prisoners took their
meals, The Kid guessed.

The air was smoky. The shaft was lit by dozens
of torches thrust into holders attached to the
walls. The Kid looked up and saw that several
ventilation holes had been drilled in the ceiling,
but there weren't enough to carry the smoke
away efficiently.

The dark, brooding stone walls, the flickering
red light from the torches, the stench of the
smoke—he could see why the tunnel was known
as Hades. Anybody who spent much time there
would feel like he was doomed—damned to the
underworld realm of Satan himself.

Some of the doors were open, leading into
empty cells. One such door was in the rear wall,
as far as it could possibly be from the light of day.
The Kid realized that was their destination.

He twisted his head to look back over his
shoulder. The oblong of light that marked the
tunnel mouth had shrunk, and it was growing
smaller with every step. The Kid felt panic coil
inside his belly like a rattlesnake.

They were going to lock him up because they
thought he was Bloody Ben Bledsoe, whoever
that was, and he would never get out of there.
Even if they didn't hang him, he would spend
the rest of his days in that hellish place, wasting

away until he was a mere shadow of himself, a dried-out husk of the man who was both Conrad Browning and Kid Morgan.

He fought down the urge to scream and thrash, to do something—anything—to stop them from putting him in that cell. He knew it wouldn't do any good. The guards would beat him into submission and then throw him in there.

And he didn't want to give them the satisfaction of seeing him lose his nerve. He was sure if he gave in to what he was feeling, the guards would tell Warden Fletcher that he had broken down.

The Kid was damned if he was going to let that happen.

So he steeled his nerves and stood up straight as they took him to the cell.

"Welcome home, Bledsoe," one of the guards jeered as they reached the door. Shoving him forward, they pitched him bodily through the opening.

He stumbled on the cell's rough stone floor but managed to stay on his feet. As he swung around, the door slammed with a boom that echoed from one end of the tunnel to the other. He heard the clatter of a key turn in the heavy lock. A moment later, a thick bar thudded into the brackets set into the rock on both sides of the door.

"Enjoy your stay," another of the guards said. Several of them laughed.

The Kid heard their footsteps going away.

He dragged in a deep breath inhaling smoke, and coughed. Turning slowly, he looked at the cell.

There was no light. The only illumination came from the reddish glow that filtered in through the small window with iron bars. As his eyes adjusted he was able to make out his surroundings. The cell was eight feet wide and ten feet deep. A narrow canvas bunk with no mattress, only a metal frame, hung from the right-hand wall. A thin, folded blanket lay on the bunk.

A small bucket stood in one corner. The Kid saw that it had water in it. A larger bucket, in another corner, was to be used to relieve himself.

That was everything in the cell. A place to sleep, a little water to drink, a bucket to answer the call of nature in.

Home, sweet home, The Kid thought bitterly.

He knew if he had to stay in there for very long, he would go mad.

Chapter 7

Footsteps approached the cell again. The Kid turned, looked out through the window, and saw the guard named Smithson coming toward him. Smithson had some sort of bundle in his arms.

He didn't unlock the door, shoving the bundle between the bars instead. It was a tight fit.

"Take your clothes off and put these on," Smithson told The Kid. "Then pass your clothes back out through the window. Boots, too."

"Is this necessary?"

"It's the rule. You'll learn pretty quick that things go easier around here if you follow the rules, Bledsoe."

The Kid picked up the bundle. He saw that it was a pair of gray wool trousers and a gray wool shirt wrapped around a pair of shoes, along with some rough underwear and socks.

Smithson pushed something else between the bars. It fell to the cell floor and landed with a clang of metal.

"When you've got the new duds on, snap those leg irons on your ankles," Smithson said.

"And if I don't?"

"Then you don't set foot outside your cell. Nobody does without the leg irons on."

"Maybe I like it in here."

"You say that now. You won't feel that way after a few days without being able to go up to the mouth of the tunnel so you can see the sun. You'll really feel like you're in Hades. The real thing, I mean."

"I know what you mean," The Kid muttered. "I already feel that way."

"Then if you know what's good for you, you'll cooperate, Bledsoe."

"I don't suppose it would do any good to tell you again that I'm not who you think I am."

"I wouldn't know a thing about that," Smithson said. "And I don't want to. Now, are you gonna put on those clothes?"

With a sigh, The Kid started taking off his own clothes.

A few minutes later, he was dressed in the drab, scratchy prison outfit. He took his boots off and put on the shoes. He pushed his clothing back through the bars, one item at a time.

"Now the irons," Smithson reminded him.

The Kid picked up the shackles and sat down on the bunk. The leg irons would make a decent weapon in a fight. The shackles themselves were heavy enough and had a short but thick length of chain between them.

But once they were snapped onto his ankles, they would be useless for anything except forcing him to shuffle along with his steps greatly restricted. That was their intended purpose, of course.

Smithson looked through the window. "If you don't put them on," he said, "you won't get to come out for chow. You'll have to live on what we can pass you through the bars. You won't get your free time. We can't even clean your slops bucket. We have to see the irons on your ankles before the door is ever unlocked. That's the way it works."

"All right, all right, blast it," The Kid said. He closed first one shackle and then the other around his ankles. "Satisfied?"

"Don't blame me, Bledsoe," Smithson said. "You're the one who robbed all those banks and killed those two guards." His voice took on a harsh edge. "They were friends of mine."

"In that case, it ought to really bother you that the wrong man is locked up. The son of a bitch who really killed them is still out there somewhere."

"One thing I've learned working in prisons," Smithson shot back. "Everybody's innocent. It's always a mistake. It was somebody else who robbed and killed. You think anybody on this side of the bars ever believes that?"

"This time it's true."

Smithson just shook his head and started to turn away.

The Kid stood up, lurched over to the door, and gripped the bars in the window. "If I'm lying, what harm could it do for the warden to send that wire I asked him to?" he demanded of the guard's back. "If he refuses to do it, maybe it's because he's afraid I'm telling the truth."

Pointing it out to Smithson probably wouldn't do any good, The Kid knew. The man was a guard, without any real power except over the prisoners. He couldn't change Fletcher's mind. The warden probably wouldn't even listen to him.

But The Kid wanted *somebody* in that hellish place to believe him. He wanted a shred of hope to cling to. Giving up and accepting the cruel twist of fate wasn't an option. He would never give up, never stop trying to figure out some way to be free again.

Smithson said without looking around, "You missed midday chow. You'll have to wait until tonight to eat. Sorry."

With that, he was gone. The Kid watched the dwindling figure until Smithson stepped out of the tunnel and passed through the gates into the sunlight.

The Kid wondered if he would ever again feel the warmth of the sun on his face.

During the long afternoon, The Kid watched through the bars and began to get an idea how things worked in Hades.

Prisoners were taken out of their cells in groups of six. They were allowed to shuffle around the tunnel with their leg irons clanking, talk to each other, smoke, and go up to the gates so they could look out. The sun didn't shine directly into the tunnel, but at least they could see it splashing its rays over the compound outside.

Each prisoner was trailed at all times by a pair of guards armed with rifles, so that when all six inmates congregated together, they were surrounded by a dozen guards. In addition, other guards were stationed here and there around the tunnel and at the entrance, plus there were those two Gatling guns guarding the gate.

Making a break for freedom seemed almost impossible. More than anything else, it would be a good way to get yourself killed in a hurry.

The Kid wondered how Bloody Ben Bledsoe had managed to escape.

While the prisoners were out of their cells, older prisoners fetched out the slops buckets and emptied them into a barrel mounted on a cart. Another cart carried a water tank used to refill the water buckets. The Kid figured the men responsible for those tasks were trusties who lived in the barracks in the compound.

Hades seemed to be reserved for the prisoners who were regarded as the most dangerous.

After fifteen minutes, the men were herded back into their cells and locked up. The process started all over again with the next six prisoners.

The Kid noticed some of the cells were skipped. The men inside them weren't let out. They were probably being punished for some infraction of Warden Fletcher's rules.

The trusties finished the chores by late afternoon.

They trundled the carts out of the tunnel once all the prisoners were locked in the cells again.

While the gates were still open, men brought in big pots of what smelled like stew and set them on the tables, along with stacks of wooden bowls. They left, and the gates were locked again.

The prisoners were let out a dozen at a time. Watched constantly by armed guards, they sat at the tables, picked up the bowls, and dipped them into the pots of stew. They had to eat with their fingers, which they did greedily, licking the last drops of juice out of the bowls.

As soon as they had finished eating, the guards put them back in their cells.

The Kid's hands tightened on the bars in the window as he thought about what it would be like to live like that day after day, month after month, year after year. The body might remain alive, but the mind and the spirit would not. They couldn't possibly survive. Even a year in there would be enough to turn a prisoner into a twisted, shambling mockery of a man, a mindless wreck.

If he couldn't convince Fletcher that there had been a mistake, that he was the wrong man . . . he'd have to find a way to escape. That was the only alternative.

When it came his turn to eat, the guards passed by his cell and opened the next one in line.

"Hey!" The Kid called through the bars. "What about me?"

One of the guards came up to the door and ordered, "Step back."

"Why?"

"Just do it, or you won't get anything to eat at all."

"I put on the damn leg irons like I was supposed to!" The Kid objected.

"For the last time, step back away from the door."

The Kid moved back and watched as the guard shoved two thick pieces of bread between the bars and let go of them so they fell to the floor just inside the door. The Kid scooped them up and said, "What the hell! This is all I get?"

"Warden's orders," the guard said as if that explained everything, and in truth, The Kid supposed it did. Jonas Fletcher's word was law at Hell Gate Prison.

The Kid sat down on the bunk and slowly ate the bread. Washing it down with water from the smaller bucket, he made the skimpy meal last as long as he could.

When he finished, he leaned back against the stone wall and watched the cell grow darker as night settled over the rugged mountains outside the prison. The torches still burned inside Hades, of course; the guards replaced them as necessary. But losing the light that had come through the mouth of the tunnel made more difference than The Kid expected.

Sometime during the long, lonely night, The Kid dozed off. He woke shivering from the cold, wrapped the thin blanket around himself, and went back to sleep.

The guards woke the prisoners early, before

dawn, and started taking them out for morning chow. The routine was the same. Trusties brought in wooden bowls and pots of what looked like oatmeal. The prisoners were taken out a dozen at a time to eat.

Once again the guards skipped The Kid's cell. He got a single piece of bread shoved through the barred window.

The midday meal was more of the same.

It was only a matter of time until the lack of decent food made him so weak he wouldn't be a threat to anybody. He suspected that was what Fletcher had in mind.

They had to let him out eventually, The Kid thought. His water bucket was almost empty, and his slops bucket was almost full.

That afternoon when the trusties came around with their carts, one of the guards unbarred and unlocked the door of The Kid's cell. Then four guards instead of the usual two stood with rifles trained on the door while one of them called for him to come out.

The Kid pushed the door open and hobbled out. He immediately started toward the mouth of the tunnel. He wanted some fresh air and light, and nothing was going to stop him.

He had to take such short steps because of the leg irons he began to worry he wouldn't reach his destination in time. It would be cruel indeed if he was almost there and the guards forced him to turn around and go back.

He made it to the gates and leaned against

one of them, holding on to the bars. The shadow of the cliff extended out about twenty feet. It was torture to be so close to the sunlight, yet unable to step out into it and let it wash over him.

"Pretty bad, isn't it?"

Chapter 8

The unexpected voice surprised The Kid, and he looked toward the prisoner who had shuffled up beside him. The man was older than him, around forty, with a lot of gray in his hair. He wasn't as gaunt as some of the other men, which meant he hadn't been there as long as they had.

He had dark hollows under his eyes, the same as all the other prisoners. It didn't take long for those to form, in that underground world. The Kid wondered if he already had them under his eyes.

"Yes, it's bad," he said. "I wouldn't have expected I'd miss standing in the sun so much, so soon."

The other prisoner grinned. "Yeah, they couldn't have designed this place any better if they wanted to punish us or something." He chuckled at his own dry humor and held out his hand. "I'm Carl Drake."

"Morgan," The Kid said as he shook Drake's

hand. The strength in Drake's grip was another indication he hadn't been there for a long time.

"I saw them bring you in yesterday. Looked like you'd had a bad time of it. Fletcher rough you up some?"

"A little," The Kid admitted.

"That bastard." Drake said the words without any real feeling in them, as if he had cursed Fletcher to the point it didn't mean much anymore.

The Kid pointed to the bandage around his head. "Fletcher didn't do this, though. A fella named Haggarty hit me with a pistol butt. *After* he'd creased me in the side with a bullet."

Drake let out a low whistle. "I've heard of Haggarty. He's a bounty hunter. A good one."

"I guess that depends on your point of view."

"Yeah, I see what you mean," Drake said with a chuckle.

Since Drake seemed talkative, The Kid indulged his curiosity. "I'd never heard of Hell Gate Prison before. How long has it been here?"

"It's been open about a year. Took a couple years of work before that to get it ready."

The Kid glanced around. "I can imagine. They had to blast out this tunnel, didn't they?"

"That's what I hear."

"That's what they did," The Kid said. "I can tell. I have some experience with mines."

"Now, me, all I know about mines is how to steal their payrolls and ore shipments." Drake grinned.

The Kid laughed softly. "That's why you're in here?"

"That and some assorted other things, most of which involved helping myself to money and gold that didn't actually belong to me."

The Kid's interest quickened. "When were you brought here?"

"Four months ago."

That ought to be long enough, The Kid thought. "Did you know a man named Bledsoe?"

"Bloody Ben? Sure, I knew him."

The Kid glanced around. Several guards were watching him intently, but none of them were standing too close. He lowered his voice and said, "Haggarty captured me thinking that I'm Bledsoe. For some reason, Fletcher believes it, too. Nothing I could say would convince him I'm not Bledsoe."

Drake's eyes widened as he looked at The Kid. "But . . . you're not Bledsoe," he said. "Yeah, there's a resemblance—put a beard on you and the two of you would almost be twins—but you're definitely not him."

A sense of excitement gripped The Kid. "Would you be willing to tell that to the warden, Drake?"

"Why, sure I would." Drake grunted and shook his head. "But do you really reckon he'd believe me?"

The Kid's spirits had lifted for a second, but dropped again. Drake was right, of course. There was no reason in the world to believe Fletcher would take the word of a convicted robber. Drake could probably insist until he was blue in the face that The Kid really wasn't Bloody Ben Bledsoe, but it wouldn't do any good.

"Hey, if you want me to try . . ." Drake went on.

The Kid shook his head. "No, it would be a waste of time. I see that now."

"You could get every man in here to swear you're not Bledsoe, and it wouldn't change Fletcher's mind. Once he's made it up, that's it."

The Kid gave a hollow laugh. "Yes, but he wants me to tell him where the loot from all of Bledsoe's robberies is hidden, and I can't do that. I don't have any idea."

"Of course not. While he was in here, Bledsoe bragged that the only one who knew was him. I reckon that's why he busted out, so he could go and get it."

The Kid knew they were running out of time. Soon the guards would start herding them back to their cells. The trusties were almost finished with their chores in the cells that were currently open.

"How in the world did Bledsoe manage to get out?" The Kid asked. "I've looked around, and I don't see any way to escape."

However Bledsoe had gotten out of Hell Gate, Fletcher had probably taken action to make sure it didn't happen again. Still, knowing how Bledsoe had managed might be a handy thing to know somewhere down the line.

"I can tell you—" Drake began.

He didn't get to finish. At that moment, a

loud, angry voice said from behind them, "I told you I'd settle that score with you, Drake. Get ready to pay up . . . in blood!"

The Kid and Drake swung around. One of the biggest, ugliest men The Kid had ever seen stood a few feet away, his hands clenched into massive, mallet-like fists. His bald head was shaped somewhat like a bullet, but it had enough lumps and depressions to show it had taken a lot of punishment over the years. He stood several inches over six feet, had shoulders like an ox-yoke, and arms like the trunks of young trees.

"Friend of yours?" The Kid asked softly.

"Not hardly," said Drake.

The man took a step toward them and said, "You didn't think I'd let you get away with double-crossin' me and the rest of the gang, did you?"

Drake shook his head. "I told you, Otto, I never double-crossed you or anybody else. I didn't have anything to do with that posse waiting for us in Raton. Somebody else in the gang must've sold us out."

"Then why were you the only one who got away?" Otto demanded.

"Just the luck of the draw," Drake said. "I tell you, I didn't do it."

Otto gave him a stubborn glare. "If it was somebody else, why did the lawdogs arrest all of us? They would've let the one who sold us out go, wouldn't they?"

"Maybe, maybe not," Drake argued. "Maybe they wanted it to look good, so they put all of you behind bars. They could've released the traitor later. I don't know where all the other members of the gang are now. Do you?"

Otto frowned as if thinking about such complex questions made his head hurt. He gave it a shake, reminding The Kid of an angry old bull.

"No, I reckon they're all scattered hell west and crosswise," he rumbled. "But I'm still mad at you, Drake."

"I'm sorry you feel that way. You don't have any reason to."

The Kid noticed the guards had been standing around, watching the confrontation to see how it was going to play out. If Otto had carried through on his obvious intention and attacked Drake, maybe the guards would have stepped in to break up the fight.

The Kid didn't know about that. He wasn't at all sure they would have.

For the moment, trouble seemed to have been averted by Drake's calm and reasonable responses to Otto's bluster. The guards moved closer, and with a jerk of his rifle, one of them ordered, "All right, back to your cells now."

The prisoners began shuffling toward the open doors of their cells. Otto cast another hard, angry glance toward Drake but didn't say anything else.

"Looks like you've got an enemy in here," The Kid commented to Drake.

"Yeah, but that's nothing unusual. It's a bad

bunch that gets sent to Hades. I'll tell you about me and Otto sometime, if you're interested."

The Kid nodded. He didn't plan to make any friends in there, but it might come in handy to have a potential ally. Carl Drake was the first person at Hell Gate Prison to believe he wasn't Bloody Ben Bledsoe. And Drake claimed to know how Bledsoe had managed to escape, which was definitely valuable knowledge.

The Kid said, "Maybe I'll see you at chow, if they ever take me off bread and water."

"They will," Drake assured him. "Just don't cause any trouble, and eventually Fletcher will get tired of it and move on to tormenting somebody else."

The Kid hoped he could wait that long.

Chapter 9

The next few days were some of the longest The Kid had ever endured. He was let out of the cell for a short time each day, but his meals still consisted of bread and water. He could feel himself growing weaker and there was nothing he could do about it.

The doctor came every day, checked his wounds, and changed the dressings. Every time Thurber was in the cell, a guard came in with him, and at least two more stood just outside the door, their rifles ready.

The white-haired physician proclaimed The Kid's injuries were healing nicely. After a couple days he left off the bandage around the head wound, saying it wasn't necessary anymore.

The Kid saw Carl Drake several times through the barred window in his door, but they weren't let out for their exercise period at the same time again. The Kid wondered if one of the guards had reported to the warden that he and Drake had been talking, and Fletcher wanted to break up any budding friendship.

On the morning of the fifth day of his imprisonment The Kid was up close to the door of his cell in order to catch the bread when it was shoved between the bars. Two guards came to the door, and one of them told him to move back away from it.

At the guard's order, he shuffled all the way to the rear wall of the cell. As he stood there, he heard the bar being removed, and a moment later a key rattled in the lock.

"You're coming out for breakfast this morning," the guard said. "Don't cause any trouble, and maybe it'll stay that way."

"Is there coffee?" The Kid asked.

"Yeah."

The Kid closed his eyes for a second and sighed in anticipation.

He hadn't been in there all that long, but already he could understand how long periods of confinement broke the spirits of a prisoner. When all the things people took for granted in their everyday lives were suddenly denied, even the smallest bit of normality was greatly magnified. The prospect of being able to sit at a table, eat breakfast, and drink coffee seemed like heaven.

Under the rifles of the two guards, he left the cell and made his laborious way to one of the tables. The coffee had already been poured in wooden cups. The prisoners weren't trusted with crockery, since it could be broken easily and the sharp edges of the pieces could be used as weapons.

The Kid grabbed a bowl, dipped it in the pot of oatmeal, and sat down at the end of the table. He forced himself not to wolf down the food or gulp the coffee. Taking his time with both, he savored the taste.

A few minutes later, someone sat down beside him. The Kid glanced over and recognized Carl Drake.

"See, I told you they'd let you out sooner or later," Drake said with a grin.

The Kid used a finger to scrape the last of the oatmeal out of the bowl. "You were right," he agreed.

"If you behave yourself, things probably won't go back to the way they were before."

The Kid didn't say anything.

Drake's forehead creased a little in a frown. "You don't plan on behaving yourself?"

"You know I'm not Bledsoe," The Kid said quietly. "They don't have any right to keep me locked up here."

"Maybe not, but they've got the bars and the guns. That sort of trumps what's right or wrong."

"Bledsoe made it out."

"Even if you escaped, you'd be a fugitive from now on."

That brought a faint smile to The Kid's face as he shook his head. "No," he corrected, "Ben Bledsoe would be the fugitive, which he already is. There are no real charges against me."

Drake grunted. "You know, I hadn't thought about it like that. You'd be free and clear . . . unless somebody mistook you for Bledsoe again."

"I'd make a point of it to get as far away from New Mexico Territory as I could."

Drake sipped his coffee and nodded. "Well, that might work," he said. "But there's a better way."

The Kid looked over at him with interest. "What are you talking about, Drake?"

"Find the real Bledsoe, bring him back, and show everybody that you're not him."

The idea was stunning in its simplicity. The Kid had some experience as a manhunter; he had tracked down the bastards responsible for Rebel's death, after all.

"How long ago did Bledsoe break out?" he asked.

"A couple weeks."

The Kid nodded. "The trail's had a chance to go cold, but I might be able to pick it up again."

"You're forgetting something."

"What's that?"

Drake smiled ruefully. "You can't pick up anybody's trail from in here."

The Kid downed the last of his coffee. "I don't plan to stay in here," he said as he set the empty cup on the table. "You're going to tell me how Bledsoe escaped. If he can do it, I can, too, and then I'll go after him."

Drake shook his head and said, "Sorry, Morgan. I'm not going to tell you anything."

Anger flashed through The Kid. He started

to say something, but Drake lifted a hand to forestall the hot words.

"I'm not going to tell you anything," Drake repeated softly, not looking at The Kid, "unless you agree that when you bust out of here, I'm going with you."

Chapter 10

For a long moment, The Kid didn't say anything. He wasn't sure he trusted Carl Drake with his life, and that was what it would amount to if he agreed to work with the man on an escape plan. Drake could betray him to Fletcher at any time.

The same thing was true of him, The Kid realized. He could turn Drake in for plotting an escape. That meant Drake was prepared to trust him. The Kid took that into consideration. "I'll think about it," he said. It was as far as he was going at the moment.

"Don't think about it too long," Drake warned. "I might take it into my head to go ahead and bust out by myself. Every day I'm in here with Otto is another day he might decide to go ahead and bust me in two."

"I thought you convinced him you didn't have anything to do with the rest of your gang getting arrested."

"Every day's a new day for Otto," Drake said. "He's not exactly what you'd call right in the head."

The Kid understood. He had seen that loco look in Otto's eyes himself. "I'll let you know," he said. "By tomorrow."

Drake scraped the last of his food from the bowl and nodded. "You do that."

Each time The Kid was out of Number One, he had studied every detail he could see about Hades, searching for some clue to the way out. He hadn't found a thing, but he kept up the effort anyway.

A few minutes later, the prisoners were taken back to their cells. The guard named Smithson was one of the pair following The Kid to his cell. Smithson said, "It won't do you any good, Bledsoe."

"What won't?" The Kid asked.

"Looking for a way out. There isn't any. We're ready now for what you pulled before."

The Kid glanced back and smiled coolly. Smithson had just summed up the main worry, but he wasn't going to let the guard see that.

An escape plan was usually good for one attempt only, especially if it was successful. Fletcher would have moved to close off whatever method the real Bledsoe had used.

Yet Drake seemed to believe they could still use Bledsoe's plan. It was an odd contradiction, one that puzzled The Kid.

Instead of pondering it, he asked Smithson a question. "Did the warden send that telegram to my lawyers the way I asked him to?"

"The warden doesn't tell me what telegrams he

sends or doesn't send," Smithson snapped. "Anyway, nobody's gonna fall for that bluff of yours, Bledsoe."

"What if it's not a bluff? What if I'm telling the truth?"

"Then I guess you're out of luck, because you're not going anywhere."

They reached the cell, and as soon as The Kid shuffled inside, the door slammed behind him. The bar thudded down into its brackets.

Those were awful sounds, and they threatened to strike despair into The Kid's heart before he stubbornly shoved the feeling away.

He couldn't afford to give in to despair. That led to surrender.

And Kid Morgan was never going to surrender.

He might have to risk taking Carl Drake up on his proposal.

Mid-morning, The Kid got a surprise. Several guards showed up at the door of his cell. As one of them unlocked it, the man said, "Step back, Bledsoe. You're coming out."

The Kid stood up from where he'd been sitting on the bunk and moved to the rear wall. "Why?" he asked through the barred window. "Am I going somewhere?"

"That's right. The warden wants to see you."

"Why?"

The guard snorted. "You think he tells us? He just said to fetch you." The bar was removed and set aside. "We're fetching you."

A key rattled in the lock, and the door swung open. The guards, except the one who had unlocked the door, had their rifles at their shoulders, aiming through the open doorway at the prisoner.

"Come on out."

Taking the short steps forced on him by the leg irons, The Kid left the cell. The guards surrounded him, and the little group started toward the mouth of the tunnel, moving slowly.

Some of the prisoners watched through the windows in their cell doors. They didn't know why he was being taken out, but they knew he would get to walk in the sunshine. They were jealous and jeered at him as he passed.

The Kid saw Carl Drake looking at him from one of the cells. Drake's forehead was creased in a frown. He appeared to be worried, and maybe with good reason. He was counting on The Kid helping him escape from Hell Gate. There was no way of knowing what was going to happen next.

The gate guards opened one of the gates, and The Kid shuffled through the gap. For the first time in days, he didn't have the stone walls of Hades looming all around and above him.

He took a deep breath, and while he couldn't actually call it the sweet air of freedom that he inhaled, not with those leg irons on, it still felt good.

The warmth of the sun on his face felt even better. Good enough, in fact, that he could almost ignore those two Gatling guns aimed at him.

Almost, but not quite.

The Kid and the guards around him walked between the Gatling gun emplacements and the barracks where the more trusted inmates lived. A moment later they reached the rear door of the admininstration building. A couple guards backed through the door, keeping their rifles trained on The Kid.

He gave them a wry smile. "You fellas must think I'm mighty dangerous."

"We haven't forgotten what happened when you busted out before, Bledsoe," one of the blue-uniformed men snapped. "We had to bury two of our friends."

The Kid didn't waste his breath denying that he'd had anything to do with those deaths. Now that he had almost a week's worth of beard stubble on his face, he probably looked more like Bloody Ben Bledsoe than ever.

The guards marched him to Warden Fletcher's office. When one of them swung the door open, it wasn't Jonas Fletcher The Kid saw sitting behind the warden's desk.

It was Fletcher's daughter Jillian.

"Miss Fletcher," the guard said in surprise. "Where's the warden?"

"He had to go over to our house," Jillian replied. "My mother sent me to get him. He'll be back shortly, I'm sure." She made a dismissive gesture. "You can leave the prisoner here. I'll keep an eye on him while we wait."

The guard frowned. "Begging your pardon, miss," he said, "but you know we can't do that."

"I don't see why not. What could he possibly do with all you guards waiting right outside the office?"

"You don't know how dangerous this man is, Miss Fletcher."

"He already has leg irons on. You could shackle his hands, too."

The guard shook his head. "Nope. I'm sorry, miss. Can't do it."

Jillian stood up and glared at the man. "For God's sake!" she said. "I'm giving you an order."

"I don't take orders from you, Miss Fletcher," the guard broke in. "I take 'em from your father."

Jillian's lips thinned angrily. "He's going to hear about this disrespect."

"You go right ahead and tell him whatever you think you need to, miss. We're still not leaving this murdering outlaw alone with you."

The Kid couldn't figure it out. Jillian had to know what a dangerous man Ben Bledsoe was. It didn't make any sense that she would want to be left alone with him.

Unless she knew that he *wasn't* Bledsoe.

The thought made him draw in a sharp breath. Did he have an unexpected ally in that place?

"All right, you can stay," Jillian said with a pout signifying that she was used to getting her own way. She pointed to the chair in front of the desk. "You might as well sit down, Mr. Bledsoe. My mother isn't well, so even though I expect my father back shortly, there's really no telling how long he'll be."

The guard closest to The Kid put a hand on his shoulder and shoved him into the chair. "Yeah, sit, Bledsoe," the man ordered. "And don't budge, if you know what's good for you."

Jillian sat down behind the desk again. The Kid said, "I'm sorry that your mother is ill, Miss Fletcher."

The guard right behind him growled, "Speak when you're spoken to, Bledsoe."

Jillian raised a hand. "No, that's all right." She looked at The Kid. "That's an odd sentiment for a prisoner to have."

The Kid shook his head and said, "Not really."

"Most of the prisoners here hate my father."

A faint smile touched The Kid's lips. "I wasn't talking about your father. I don't have any grudge against your mother. I've never even met the lady. What's wrong with her?"

"Bledsoe . . ." the guard said warningly.

"No, really, it's all right," Jillian told him. She addressed The Kid again. "She has consumption. Father thought the air here in New Mexico might help her, but so far it hasn't."

"I'm sorry to hear that. If your father would get in touch with my lawyers in San Francisco, they might be able to recommend a specialist who could help your mother. They donate a considerable amount of money to various hospitals around the country in my mother's name, so they know a lot of doctors."

The guard couldn't stand it anymore. "Blast it, Bledsoe!" he burst out. "Stop spouting that hogwash!"

Jillian stared across the desk. "You're very well-spoken for an inmate. What happened to your mother?"

The Kid folded his hands in his lap and said calmly, "She was murdered by outlaws, the sort of men that everyone around here seems to think I am. If you really knew me, you'd know how preposterous that is."

Without meaning to, he had hit on a new strategy in his effort to get out of there. If he could convince Fletcher that he wasn't Ben Bledsoe, he wouldn't have to break out, with Drake or anybody else. The first step in convincing Fletcher might be to convince the warden's daughter, and he thought she already had doubts about his identity.

So they all thought he was some barely literate outlaw, did they?

He would have to show them how wrong they were. He hadn't spent years at the finest universities back east for nothing. A few quotations from the classics ought to be a good start, maybe even throw in a few phrases of Latin . . .

But before he could continue impressing Jillian with how educated and erudite he was, Jonas Fletcher roared from the office doorway, "What the hell is going on here?"

Chapter 11

Jillian looked up sharply, a frightened expression on her face, and started to get to her feet.

At the same time, the guard standing immediately behind The Kid's chair turned toward Fletcher. "You said to bring Bledsoe in here, Warden," the man said. "We fetched him from Hades, but when we got here, you'd stepped out of the office for a minute—"

"Then why did you bring him in here where my daughter was?" Fletcher stalked over to the desk and pointed toward Jillian with a finger that shook angrily.

"We didn't know Miss Fletcher was in here, sir," the guard explained.

"Didn't one of the clerks tell you?"

The guard shook his head. "None of the clerks were at their desks when we came in."

Fletcher threw his hands in the air. "Incompetents!" he said. "I'm surrounded by incompetents!" He whirled on Jillian, who shrank back into the chair. "And you! What do you mean by staying here in my office? I thought you were going with me back to the house. I was halfway there before I realized you weren't just lagging behind. You were nowhere to be seen!"

Jillian was clearly afraid of her father, but her chin tilted up with defiance as she said, "I couldn't stand it anymore. You leave me over there to take care of her, to watch as she coughs her life out and wastes away to nothing. I just had to get out for a few minutes!"

Fletcher tilted his head to the side, as if he couldn't believe what he had just heard. In a low, dangerous voice, he said, "By God, girl, don't take that tone of voice with me."

"Why not?" she challenged him. "Are you going to throw me into Hades with the rest of the damned souls?"

Fletcher looked thunderstruck that she would say such a thing to him. For a long moment he didn't make any reply. Then he grated, "Go back to the house. Your mother needs you."

"Of course she does," Jillian said as she stood up. "Lord knows she won't get any real comfort from her husband while she's dying."

For a second, The Kid thought Fletcher was going to slap her. The muscles in the man's arm trembled with the all-too-evident urge to strike out.

The Kid wasn't sure what he would do if that happened. Could he sit by and allow any man to hit a woman, even his own daughter? Especially a bastard like Fletcher? The Kid knew even with leg irons on, he was fast enough to get out of his chair and grab Fletcher's arm before a blow could fall.

It would probably get him a good beating from the guards if he did.

Thankfully, he didn't have to make that decision. With a visible effort, Fletcher brought his rage under control. "Get out," he rasped at Jillian.

She left, scurrying out of the office, but not before casting a sympathetic glance toward The Kid.

She probably had good reason to be sympathetic, he thought. Fletcher was even angrier than he would have been if none of that had happened.

The Kid stayed put as the warden went behind the desk and lowered himself wearily into the chair. "Bledsoe," Fletcher said as he looked across the desk. "Have you changed your mind?"

"About what?" The Kid asked. "The fact that I'm not Bloody Ben Bledsoe?"

Fletcher's mouth quirked in a cold smile. "Still harping on that, are you? Give it up. With that beard, you look even more like your old self now than you did when Haggarty brought you here." Fletcher leaned forward and clasped his hands together on the desk. "No, I was talking about the loot from all those robberies you pulled."

The Kid shook his head. "I don't know a thing about it."

"You're a damned fool. You know you'll never

get out of here again. That money can't do you any good now. The only possible benefit you might get from it is if you reveal where it is. That might get you a little clemency somewhere along the way."

"Or get me hanged," The Kid shot back. "Like Haggarty said, those bankers won't let me be convicted of murder and strung up as long as there's a chance they might get their money back. But once they do, they won't give a damn about me. Telling you where the money is would be the same thing as signing my death warrant." He shook his head. "But it's all moot anyway, because I don't know where the money is. I'm not Bledsoe."

Behind The Kid, one of the guards muttered to another, "What's moot?"

Fletcher's eyes narrowed. "Being stubborn's not going to do you any good."

"On the contrary, it's all I have left," The Kid said. "Except . . ."

He might as well go ahead and play the only card remaining in his hand, he decided, the one he had started to trot out when Jillian was in there.

"Did Ben Bledsoe know Latin?" he asked. "*Cogito, ergo sum.*"

"Did he say that's Sioux?" the guard whispered to his companion. He fell silent as Fletcher glared at him.

Fletcher returned his attention to The Kid.

"Well, now, that's mighty fancy talk. Do you know what it means?"

"'I think, therefore I am'," The Kid quoted. "Or *veni, vidi, vici* . . . I came, I saw, I conquered."

"So you think by throwing around a few Latin phrases, you're going to convince me you're not Ben Bledsoe?" Fletcher asked. He seemed amused, which didn't make The Kid feel any better. "Is that the idea?"

"How many outlaws would know something like that?"

"Not many, I'll grant you," Fletcher replied. "But Bledsoe would, since before he took up the owlhoot trail, he was Professor Benjamin Bledsoe and taught law at William and Mary in Virginia."

It was The Kid's turn to be thunderstruck. It was impossible that he could have predicted such an unlikely turn of events.

Life was full of bizarre happenstances. Hadn't he turned out to be the son of one of the most famous gunfighters in the West? After years as a businessman, hadn't he taken up the gun himself and carved out a reputation as an hombre who was slick on the draw and deadly accurate with a Colt?

"I didn't know that about Bledsoe," he said softly.

"Here's something else you don't know," Fletcher said as he came to his feet. "I'm tired of pussyfooting around with you, mister. We're going to end this." He jerked a hand at the guards. "Take him outside. Get his shirt off him and tie him to the whipping post."

The Kid's eyes widened in surprise. He hadn't seen a whipping post when he was first brought in to Hell Gate Prison, but he hadn't been in good shape then, either. He could have overlooked it.

The idea that Fletcher intended to have him whipped was both horrifying and repellent. He shot to his feet and exclaimed, "You can't do that!"

"I can do anything I want," Fletcher said coldly. "I'm the warden here. Inside this prison, my word is law, and you should have thought of that before you defied me, Bledsoe."

One of the guards took hold of The Kid's arm. "Come on," he said. "Don't make this any worse than it has to be."

"This is inhuman!" The Kid raged, still looking across the desk at the warden.

"So is robbing banks. So is murdering guards." Fletcher gave a curt nod. "Take him."

Another guard reached for The Kid's other arm, but before he could grasp it, The Kid suddenly twisted and struck out at the man already holding him. His fist whipped around and crashed into the guard's jaw, knocking him loose.

The Kid lunged forward, trying to get across the desk so that he could reach Fletcher. He thought wildly that if he could get his hands on the warden, he might be able to force the guards to back off. With Fletcher as his hostage, he might even be able to bluff his way out of there by threatening to kill the warden.

At the moment, he wasn't too sure it would be a bluff.

But Fletcher was ready for him. The man's hand closed around a heavy paperweight on the desk and brought it up with blinding speed. The paperweight smashed against the side of The Kid's head and knocked him sprawling on top of the desk.

The next instant, several pairs of strong hands grabbed him and jerked him upright. A fist hit him low in the back. The kidney punch sent pain stabbing through him. He gasped and arched his back, and as he did, another fist buried itself in his belly.

The Kid doubled over, wracked by pain and nausea. The wound in his side wasn't completely healed, and the struggle opened it up again. He felt the wet heat of fresh blood flowing.

Another punch hammered into him. His knees gave out, and he would have fallen if the guards hadn't been surrounding him and pummeling him at close range.

"Enough!" The word lashed out from Fletcher. "He doesn't have any more fight in him. Get him out of here and string him up to the post! I'll be out there in a minute to deal with him myself."

One of the guards began, "Warden, are you sure you don't want one of us to—"

"I said I'd deal with him myself!" Fletcher roared. "It's time this outlaw scum was taught a lesson . . . and by God, I'm going to enjoy doing the teaching!"

Chapter 12

Still stunned, The Kid was aware the guards were dragging him outside, but he couldn't summon the strength to fight anymore. His muscles wouldn't obey his commands.

The toes of his shoes plowed furrows in the dust as the guards hauled him around one of the barracks. He saw a thick beam standing upright in the ground. About fifty yards past it, backed up to the stone wall that ran all around the prison, was a small, squarish house built of rocks. It was probably Fletcher's residence, The Kid thought as his brain began to function better.

His head ached intolerably from the blow with the paperweight. He tried to ignore the pain. He had a choice of agonies: his head, his belly, his kidneys, the wound in his side . . .

They reached the upright beam that served as a whipping post. A metal hook was attached to it about seven feet above the ground. The Kid had a pretty good idea what it was for.

A couple guards grabbed his shirt and ripped it off. In other circumstances, the warmth of the sun would have felt good on his bare chest and back.

The Kid knew what was coming, but was too battered to fight back. Outnumbered as he was, it wouldn't have done much good to put up a fight. He regretted not being able to plant his fist right in the middle of some of those smug faces surrounding him.

One of the guards snapped a pair of shackles around his wrists. They were connected by a short length of chain. A longer length was also attached to the shackles. Another guard took it and tossed it over the hook above The Kid's head. He pulled on it and forced The Kid to raise his arms.

The Kid wound up facing the post with his arms stretched above his head as far as he could reach. At the same time, he had been forced up on his toes so that his stance was painfully awkward and a lot of weight was on his shoulder sockets. He felt his bones and muscles groaning under the strain.

He twisted his head to look at the men around him and rasped, "You know this isn't right. Some of you have to know I'm not Bledsoe."

"We just do our jobs, mister," one of the guards said.

"You look a hell of a lot like that bastard Bledsoe to me," another put in.

They began to move back, and even though The Kid couldn't see Fletcher, he knew the warden was coming.

Fletcher circled the post so he could look at The Kid. He had taken off his coat and tie, but still wore his vest. His shirtsleeves were rolled up a couple of turns. He carried a coiled blacksnake whip in his right hand.

Fletcher glared at The Kid and said, "I'd tell you that you have one last chance to avoid this by admitting where you stashed the loot, Bledsoe, but it would be a lie. You're getting this whipping no matter what you tell me now. You've got it coming." He paused. "Still, I might be inclined to be a little more merciful if you cooperate."

"I can't tell you something I don't know," The Kid said between gritted teeth. "The only thing I have to say to you, Fletcher is . . . go to hell."

That show of defiance brought a smile to the warden's face. "You're about to be more convinced than ever that's where you are," he said softly.

He let go of the whip except for the handle. It uncoiled and slithered around his feet with a sinister whisper. Nodding slowly, Fletcher moved out of The Kid's line of sight again.

Silence hung over Hell Gate as The Kid waited.

The first strike didn't come without warning. The Kid heard Fletcher's grunt of effort and had a split second to close his eyes and steel himself for the lashing impact. The whip struck him at an angle across the back and cut into his skin and flesh, leaving behind a streak of hellish fire that made The Kid surge forward against the post. He panted as agony coursed through him.

"That's just the beginning," Fletcher warned.

With a snake-like hiss, the whip retreated, then sprang forward again as Fletcher wielded it with a cruel, efficient touch. He jerked it back so the weighted tip popped just as it touched The Kid's left shoulder blade. The Kid bit back a yell of pain as the tip gouged out a chunk of flesh.

The song of the whip continued its grim tune. Fletcher varied his brutality, moving the black-snake around so that it left a criss-crossing grid of bloody stripes on The Kid's back, which was also dotted with wounds from the tip that oozed crimson. At first The Kid tried to hold himself upright, but as the torment continued, the sea of pain in which he found himself engulfed him so completely that all he could do was hang limply from the shackles attached to the whipping post.

Somewhere in his brain, a part of his mind numb to the agony wondered if the prisoners inside the cavern called Hades could hear what was going on. They couldn't see it—the whipping post was shielded from the tunnel mouth by one of the barracks—but it was so quiet in the prison compound they had to be able to hear the whip popping and slashing.

He wanted to scream in agony, and the prisoners would have been able to hear those cries for sure. He swallowed the cries again and again, because he didn't want to give Fletcher the satisfaction of hearing them, but the screams were coming closer and closer to escaping.

"That son of a bitch!"

The Kid's eyes snapped open at the sound of the familiar voice. He saw her standing in front of him, a look of fierce anger on her face. She wore jeans and a buckskin shirt, and her hat hung behind her head by its chin strap. Her thick blond hair fell to her shoulders and framed her beautiful face. She looked much like she had the first time he had met her, right down to the holstered six-gun strapped around her hips.

"Rebel," he whispered.

"Don't let that bastard win, Conrad. If I could, I'd plug the varmint right between the eyes. You'll have to do it for me. Promise me you will, one of these days, Conrad."

"I . . . I promise," The Kid husked between lips that he had bitten bloody to hold back the screams.

She moved a step closer to him and held up a hand. *"I miss you so much."* She reached toward him, as if she wanted to brush her fingers across his cheek.

He ached for her touch, strained forward so that for the first time in more than a year, the two of them could make contact. He wished he could kiss her. He knew the sweetness of her lips would take away all his pain.

Though they strained toward each other, she couldn't quite seem to touch him. An expression of deep sadness came over her face.

"I have to go now, Conrad."

"No!" he cried hoarsely. "No, don't go! Don't leave me again!" The words were in his mind. He didn't know only incoherent croaking sounds were coming from his mouth.

"Be strong, Conrad. Don't let him win. You have to get out of here. You have to get out . . ."

She was gone, and the strength he had drawn from

the sight of her disappeared with her. Bitterness flooded through him. She hadn't really been there at all, he realized. She hadn't returned to him, however briefly, from beyond the wall of tragedy and death. It was all his feverish imagination. It was over, all over, and despair welled up inside him . . .

Something cool touched his face.

Something smooth and soft and comforting.

The hand of the woman he loved.

It was a fleeting thing, there and then gone, but it was enough. Even in his terrible state, The Kid knew some things should not be questioned, only accepted, embraced, clung to with the power of hope and love.

His faith was restored.

And with it came a terrible thirst for justice and vengeance.

His head fell forward, and darkness closed around him.

He barely heard the screams, followed by angry shouts. He had no idea what was going on, and he didn't care. As the darkness took him, his final thought was that he wasn't defeated. Not yet.

Not as long as he still drew breath and still loved Rebel Callahan Browning.

And that would be forever.

Chapter 13

He woke up to the touch of something cool on his face, but it was a wet cloth, not ghostly fingers.

It felt good. The Kid sighed as he embraced that slight bit of comfort and tried to ignore the terrible pains that wracked the rest of his body.

"You're awake, eh?" The voice belonged to the old, white-haired doctor. Thurber went on, "Just lie still, Bledsoe. You don't want to be moving around much, and you sure as hell don't want to roll over onto your back."

The Kid's tongue felt swollen to twice its normal size as he worked it out of his mouth and swiped it over dry lips. That didn't help much, since his tongue was parched, too, but after a moment he was able to say, "Wh-where . . ."

"You're in the infirmary," Thurber supplied when The Kid couldn't go on. "The warden wanted to throw you back in your cell, but I told him you'd die if he did that."

"Th-thanks," The Kid whispered.

"Oh, it wasn't a lie. He beat you to within an inch of your life, and that inch would have slipped away without the proper care. You lost so much blood from your back and from the wound in your side that opened up again, there was a puddle of the stuff around your feet when they brought me to the whipping post. I cleaned you up and did what I could for you, but I'm afraid you're going to have some scars on your back."

The Kid might have laughed if he hadn't been so weak. He didn't give a damn about scars. He already had plenty of scars on his soul that would never heal. A few stripes on his flesh didn't matter.

He lifted his head a little so he could look around. He was lying facedown on a narrow mattress on an iron bedstead, in a room with bare walls and a single high window with iron bars set into it. Several other beds were in the room, but they were empty.

The Kid still had the shackles on his wrists, and when he moved his feet slightly, he heard the leg irons clank. "Don't they know I'm . . . too beat up to . . . go anywhere?" he asked Thurber, who sat beside the bed in a ladderback chair.

"They know, but it's the warden's orders that the irons stay on. He's not taking any chances with you, whoever you are."

It took a couple heartbeats for the implication of the doctor's words to penetrate The Kid's brain. When they did, his head jerked up, causing a fresh burst of pain that made him wince. He ignored it and said, "What do you mean? You know I'm not Ben Bledsoe?"

Instead of answering directly, Thurber reached out and brushed back the longish hair that hung over The Kid's left ear.

"What happened here?" he asked.

The top of the ear was gone, leaving an odd-looking area covered by a healed-over scar.

The Kid closed his eyes for a second and cursed himself. He had gotten so used to his ear being mutilated that he never even thought about it anymore. It hadn't occurred to him that the old injury could prove he wasn't Bledsoe.

"An outlaw used his knife to cut off part of my ear while he and his gang were holding me for ransom," he said after a moment. Frank Morgan had gotten him out of that deadly jam, and it was the start of the thaw between father and son.

"When did that happen?"

"Years ago," The Kid said. Despite the terrible shape he was in, he felt excitement surge inside him. "Go get Fletcher and show it to him. That'll prove I'm not Bledsoe!" A thought came to him. "Unless . . . no, that's crazy."

But he thought it was crazy that the outlaw who looked so much like him could speak Latin. "Bledsoe's ear doesn't look like this, does it?" he asked in a hollow voice.

Thurber chuckled. "It didn't when he busted out of here. There's no telling what might've happened to him while he was gone. It was more than a month before you were caught and brought back here, you know."

"The wound on my ear is a lot older than a month."

"Well, it looks older than that to me, all right," Thurber replied with a shrug. "But you have to understand, I can't *prove* that it is."

"Of course you can! It's your medical opinion. It's *proof.* It would stand up in a court of law."

Thurber shook his head. "In case you haven't figured it out yet, my friend, in this place, if it doesn't convince Warden Fletcher, it doesn't prove a damn thing."

The Kid knew that was true, but now that he had a straw at which to grasp, he wasn't going to give it up. "You can tell him," he said. "You have to tell him."

"Maybe I will. But even if I do, I've got a hunch it won't really matter."

The Kid groaned in a mixture of pain and disappointment, then he thought of another possibility. "Tell Miss Fletcher."

Thurber frowned. "Jillian? Why would I want to do that?"

"Because she already has doubts that I'm Bledsoe. Convince her of the truth, and then both of you can try to persuade her father that I'm not lying."

The doctor shook his head. "Sorry, but I'm not saying anything to that girl. The warden doesn't like it when she takes any interest in the prisoners. Doesn't like it one little bit. Getting her involved any more than she already is would just turn him against you that much more."

Something about Thurber's voice prompted The Kid to ask, "What do you mean, any more than she already is?"

The doctor's fingers rasped on the white stubble on his chin. "That's right, you'd passed out by then," he said. "I guess Jillian found out somehow what was going on. She came running out, screaming at her father, and tried to take the whip away from him. He raised holy hell right back at her and told her she was forbidden to leave their house." Thurber shook his head. "That won't sit well with her. That young lady has a mind of her own, and she doesn't mind expressing it."

The Kid had seen evidence of it with his own eyes. He still thought Jillian Fletcher would be a good ally to have, along with the doctor. But he supposed the effort to enlist her help could wait. Given the shape he was in, he wouldn't be going anywhere for a while. He would have to heal up some first.

"What happens now?" he asked.

"You lay there and let that medicine I spread on your back do its work, that's what happens now," Thurber said. "I cleaned the wound in your side, took some stitches in it, and bandaged it again. Maybe it'll stay closed better this time. I hope so."

The Kid shifted his legs. They wouldn't move very far.

"I'm chained to the bed, aren't I?"

"Yes, but you don't need to go anywhere. You need to rest."

"For how long?"

"You'll be here for a few days, anyway. Maybe a week or more." Thurber got to his feet. "Just don't get any fancy ideas about taking advantage and trying to get away. There are two guards right outside the door, and will be that many around the clock as long as you're here."

The Kid glanced at the window. It was too small for him to get his head through, let alone his body. It let a little air and light into the room, and that was all.

"I still wish you'd say something to Fletcher about my ear," he said.

"I'll think about it," Thurber replied with another shrug, "but I can't guarantee anything." He lowered his voice. "I don't want to get on the warden's bad side any more than anybody else around here does."

"He's a lunatic. A cruel, ruthless lunatic. You know that, don't you?"

"I don't know anything," Thurber said, "except that I want to draw my pay and not bring any trouble down on my head. That's what I know . . . Bledsoe." He left the room.

As the door closed and Thurber's footsteps faded away, The Kid fought once more against the feelings of helplessness and despair welling up inside him and painfully tightening his chest. That one brief moment of hope had faded, but he couldn't forget what he had seen and heard while he was chained to the whipping post. Rebel had come to him to offer hope and encouragement and extract a promise from him.

A promise that someday he would shoot Jonas Fletcher right between the eyes.

The Kid had to live in order to keep that promise. He couldn't give up, no matter how hopeless things looked. "Stay with me, Rebel," he whispered to the empty room. "Stay with me."

Though there was no sound, he seemed to hear her speaking soft words of comfort to him.

Chapter 14

Kid Morgan was in the infirmary at Hell Gate Prison for ten days. Part of that time, he suffered from a fever brought on by infection from his numerous wounds. Dr. Thurber said the fever had to run its course, and eventually it did, breaking during the night. When The Kid woke in the morning, his bedding was drenched from the cold sweat that had leached the sickness out of him.

By the time the guards came to take him back to Hades, he was weaker than a mountain lion cub, but his head was clear. The wounds on his back had scabbed over, and after examining them that morning, Thurber had declared they were healing nicely. So was the bullet gash in his side. The cut on his head from Haggarty's gun was all right now, leaving only a small scar.

"Try not to get in any more trouble," Thurber advised before the guards took The Kid out.

"You've already lost more than your share of blood."

The Kid nodded. His beard was full, which he supposed made him look more like Bloody Ben Bledsoe than ever. He was convinced Thurber doubted he was the outlaw, and so did Jillian Fletcher. It would have been a good start on ultimately winning his freedom.

But he wasn't going to wait for that. The whipping he'd received at the hands of Jonas Fletcher convinced him the warden would never believe him, and as had been pointed out to him more than once, Fletcher's word was law. If he stayed in Hell Gate for the months or years it might take to get out through legal means, Fletcher would kill him.

He had to escape as soon as he had his full strength back. There was no other answer.

When the guards marched him into Hades, the man-made cavern was empty except for other guards. The prisoners were locked up in their cells. The Kid wanted to talk to Carl Drake as soon as he could, but he'd have to wait for that opportunity.

He walked slowly into the Number One cell, the door of which stood open waiting for him. When The Kid was inside, one of the guards said, "Next time the warden asks you a question, Bledsoe, maybe you better answer him."

The Kid sat down on his bunk and didn't say anything. He was tired of arguing with those people.

The door slammed shut, the lock rattled as the key turned in it, and the bar thudded down in its brackets.

Home, sweet home, The Kid thought bitterly.

He half expected he'd be put back on bread and water, but when evening rolled around he was taken out of the cell for supper. He shuffled to the tables, got a bowl of stew, and sat down to eat.

A minute later, Drake appeared beside him and sat down without waiting to be invited.

"How are you doing, Kid?" Drake asked in a low voice.

The Kid jerked his head in a curt nod. "I've been better," he said, "but I reckon I've been worse."

"Hard to believe anybody could be worse off than you were after that whipping, without being dead."

The Kid glanced over at him. "You couldn't see what happened from in here."

"No, but some of the trusties could from their barracks. They talked about it a little, when the guards couldn't hear. They said Fletcher whipped you until your back was nothing but blood."

"It wasn't quite that bad," The Kid said with a slight shrug. "Plenty bad enough, though."

"To tell you the truth, I figured we'd never see you again in here. Word filtered in that you were healing up, but I wasn't gonna believe it until I saw you with my own eyes." Drake regarded The Kid intently. "You don't look very good . . . but that's still a whole heap better than dead."

The Kid lifted his bowl of stew, drank some of the juice, and licked his lips. "You still want to get out of here?" he asked in a half whisper.

Drake leaned forward. "Of course I do! You want to throw in with me?"

"As soon as I get my strength back," The Kid said. "Then, whatever you have in mind, as long as it stands a decent chance of getting me out of here, count me in."

"All right," Drake said softly. "All right. Now you're talking. The two of us can make it. I know we—"

He didn't get to finish that declaration of confidence. Two massive hands came down on his shoulders, jerked him off the bench, and slung him across the stone floor of Hades. "I told you I'd get even with you for double-crossin' us!" Otto roared as he stomped after Drake.

"Otto, no!" Drake cried as he came up on one knee after rolling over a couple times. "I didn't—"

Otto wasn't listening, and as The Kid looked on, he knew that in his current condition, he couldn't do anything to stop the huge, bullet-headed outlaw. Otto drew back a big foot and swung it at Drake in a vicious kick.

Drake ducked under the kick, which would have broken his jaw if it had landed. He reached up and grabbed Otto's foot, heaving and twisting as he surged up from the ground.

Otto yelled as he windmilled his arms and went over backward. He landed on one of the tables, scattering men and bowls of stew. His shoulder hit the pot, upset it, and sent hot stew splashing in the laps of a couple prisoners.

With angry shouts, the men jumped him and started pounding him. Drake crowded in and joined the effort.

Before they could do much real damage to Otto, several guards arrived and began pulling the men away from him. Rifle butts slashed, knocking the struggling prisoners apart. Other guards leveled their weapons and yelled for the prisoners to get on the ground. The fight was broken up quickly.

Otto clambered to his feet, still blustering threats, but he had to back away with the muzzles of the guards' rifles threatening him. He pointed a long, blunt finger at Drake and said, "This ain't over, you bastard. It ain't over by a long shot."

Drake came back to the table where The Kid sat and lowered himself to the bench. He looked shaken. A grim chuckle came from him as he reached for his bowl of stew that was still sitting on the table. "You see what it's like," he said quietly. "I knew something like this was going to happen sooner or later. I'm just lucky he didn't bust my skull open or break my back before somebody stopped him. You can see why it's important to me that we get out of here just as soon as we can. It's my life we're talking about."

"Mine, too," The Kid said, thinking about what Fletcher had done to him. "I'll let you know as soon as I'm strong enough."

"Make it soon," Drake said, nodding. "Very soon."

Chapter 15

Another week went by, although it seemed more like a year to The Kid. He regained some of his strength. The meager, monotonous rations and the lack of exercise made it difficult for him to recover fully. The delay gave him a chance to talk to Drake several times, and during those conversations, The Kid began to understand how Ben Bledsoe had gotten out of that hellhole.

"I reckon you've noticed it doesn't get real smoky in here, even with those torches burning all the time," Drake said as he and The Kid sat at tables eating the breakfast gruel one morning.

Drake didn't look at The Kid as he spoke, and he kept his voice low. The guards discouraged too much conversation among the prisoners.

"Yeah," The Kid replied, also without looking at his companion. "There are vent holes drilled in the ceiling, all the way to the top of the cliff, I suppose."

"That's not all. There aren't enough of those

holes to carry all the smoke away. But back in the corner, there's a natural chimney. They either uncovered it when they were blasting this place out, or the blasting itself opened a crack in the earth that runs all the way to the surface."

The Kid frowned. "I haven't seen anything like that. And I've been looking."

"That's because the way the wall juts out and curves around, you can't spot it if you're more than three or four feet from it—especially as bad as the light is in here. Look for a spot where a couple guards are always standing, not moving, and that's where it is."

"Fletcher keeps guards there all the time?"

"Yeah."

"Then how did Bledsoe get past them?"

A guard wandered closer to them, prompting both men to fall silent. A few moments later they were marched them back to their cells, so The Kid and Drake weren't able to finish talking about Bledsoe's escape.

Their next opportunity to discuss it came the following day. Drake picked up the story where he'd left off. "One of the trusties smuggled in a knife to Bledsoe. He got out of his cell one night by pretending to be sick."

The Kid grunted. "I'm surprised any of the guards fell for that old trick."

"It wasn't a trick. The trustie smuggled in something he stole from Doc Thurber that made Bledsoe puke his guts out. That didn't stop him from knifing a guard, getting his hands on a rifle, and shooting his way past the men at the chimney. He started climbing out."

"Why didn't the guards who were still down here just shoot up the chimney and stop him?"

"Because it takes a sharp bend about twenty feet in. Bledsoe must've gotten around that bend before they could open fire. They tried ricocheting some slugs up the chimney, until Fletcher got here and ordered them to stop. He didn't want Bledsoe killed, just stopped."

"Because of the loot," The Kid murmured.

"What?"

The Kid shook his head. "Go on."

"There's not much else to say," Drake continued with a shrug. "Bledsoe climbed all the way to the top and got out. That's the last anybody's seen of him. Nobody knows for sure if he was wounded. They found some blood in the chimney, but that could've been from the guard whose throat he cut."

"Why didn't—"

Again the discussion was interrupted by a guard, but it was resumed at breakfast the next morning.

"Why didn't Fletcher send men up top to be waiting for Bledsoe when he got there?" The Kid finished his question from the day before.

"He tried, but because of the terrain, it takes about twenty minutes for anybody to get from here to the top of the cliff. By the time they got there, Bledsoe was out and gone."

"One of the guards told me they'd closed off Bledsoe's escape route."

Drake nodded. "Yeah. Fletcher has two men up there around the clock now. I've heard rumors that he's considered walling up the crack down here, but he doesn't want to do that because it vents so much of the smoke."

"That smoke would make the climb pretty bad," The Kid mused.

"Yeah, but breathing smoke for a little while is a lot better than being stuck in here."

The Kid couldn't argue with that.

"So if both ends of that natural chimney are guarded now," he said, "I don't see how you plan for us to use it to get out."

Drake smiled. "I didn't say it'd be easy. The trick is to take the boys up top by surprise. We can deal with them if they don't know we're coming."

The Kid frowned and shook his head. That didn't answer his question at all. "How do you figure on doing that?"

"We have to get out of our cells and kill the guards on this end without raising a ruckus."

The Kid sighed in exasperation. "You're still not telling me anything."

"Otto's going to provide a distraction for us."

That took The Kid by surprise. "How's he going to do that? And why would he help you? He hates you."

"Not right now, he doesn't. You have to understand. Otto's like a little kid. One day he can want to wring your neck, and the next you can talk him into being your best friend, if you know how to handle him. I know how to handle him."

"You're putting a lot of faith in that," The Kid pointed out.

"I've always been a good planner. The gang I led pulled off some complicated jobs."

The Kid grunted again and glanced at Drake. "Yes, I can tell what a good planner you are by the fact that you're in here with me."

"Hey, everybody runs out of luck sooner or later, no matter how good they are. You want to hear the rest of this or not?"

"Yeah," said The Kid. "Go ahead."

"Otto's going to start a big ruckus at breakfast tomorrow, big enough that all the guards except the two at the chimney will have to pitch in to stop him. That's when we'll jump them, take their guns, and climb out . . . if you think you're up to it. If you're not, I'll talk to Otto and try to get him to wait. That might not be easy, though."

"I'm up to it," The Kid said. "But won't those guards see us coming as we're shuffling along toward them?"

"We'll move faster than that." Drake rested a closed hand on the table and opened it part of the way for a second, just enough for The Kid to catch a glimpse of a small key. "That'll unlock our leg irons."

"How'd you get that?"

"One of the trusties stole it while he was cleaning the guards' barracks. He smuggled it in here in a pot of oatmeal. I made sure I got to the pot first and knew where to dip my bowl."

"The same trustie who smuggled the knife to Bledsoe?"

"No, that fella, well, he met with an accident not long after that, I heard. I figure Fletcher probably killed him with his bare hands."

"How did you get this one to go along with the scheme?" The Kid asked.

"It was easy enough. His brother was the one who helped Bledsoe escape. He doesn't care about anything anymore except getting back at Fletcher."

"What about Otto?"

Drake smiled. "I promised that once we escaped, we'd put together a gang and break him out, too. Of course, that's not going to happen."

The Kid felt bad about taking advantage of the dimwitted brute like that, but he knew Otto was a ruthless killer, so he wasn't going to worry much about it. "It still sounds like an awful long shot to me," he said.

"Nobody claimed it'd be easy. But it's your best chance to get out of here. If you'd rather stay and see what happens the next time Fletcher takes it into his head to beat what he wants out of you, you're welcome to do it."

The Kid gave a tiny shake of his head. "I didn't say that. I'm with you, Drake. I just don't want us to get killed."

"Even if we do, it's better than being locked up in here for the next twenty years or more," Drake said fervently. "You really want to do that? You think you could make it that long?"

The Kid knew he wouldn't make it a year in Hell Gate, let alone twenty.

"Anyway, say you make it and they finally let you go when you're an old man. You'd have nothing and nobody and the only thing you could do would be to crawl off somewhere and die. Is that what you want?"

"No," The Kid whispered.

"Then stick with me. We'll get out. I know it."

The Kid took a deep breath and let it out in a sigh. "Tomorrow morning, you say?"

"That's right. Will you be ready?"

"I'll be ready," The Kid said.

Chapter 16

As he lay on his bunk after waking up the next morning, The Kid took stock of himself. His wounds were healed for the most part, although a few small scabs remained here and there. His head was clear. He wished he were a bit stronger, but he knew that wasn't going to happen until he escaped from Hell Gate and could get some better food, along with fresh air and sunshine.

And a razor to scrape the damn beard off his face, he thought. He didn't want to resemble Bloody Ben Bledsoe anymore.

As he sat up, he thought about everything he and Drake had discussed the day before. Drake's plan still struck him as sketchy, but The Kid hadn't been able to come up with anything else.

There was one major flaw that Drake hadn't mentioned. The whole thing wouldn't work unless both he and Drake were in the same group when the guards brought the prisoners out for breakfast. Otto had to be out of his cell then, as well.

The three of them were often in the same bunch, but not always. The Kid put his shoes on and went to the little barred window in the door to watch what was going on outside.

The guards were already taking some of the prisoners out of their cells. As The Kid looked on, Drake's cell was unlocked. The guards worked their way closer to the rear wall of Hades. Otto came out and shuffled sullenly toward the mess tables, surrounded by guards.

Two out of three, The Kid thought. Now if they just came for him . . .

A minute later, a couple guards approached The Kid's cell. They set the bar aside, and a key rattled in the lock.

"Back off," one of them snapped at The Kid, who was already moving away from the door. He didn't want to give them any excuse for deciding to leave him in his cell.

He came out when they told him to and walked slowly toward the tables. Otto had taken a seat at the table closest to the tunnel mouth, while Drake was at the one farthest back . . . and closest to the natural rock chimney that was their escape route out of there.

Without being too noticeable, The Kid glanced toward the place Drake had told him about. He couldn't spot any opening in the rock wall, but he did see a couple guards standing in that area with rifles tucked under their arms. They didn't move while the other guards were bringing out the prisoners for breakfast.

That had to be it, The Kid thought. There was no other reason for those guards to be back there in the far rear corner of Hades.

The guards let prisoners sit where they wanted to during meals as long as they didn't cause any trouble. None of them paid any attention as The Kid drifted over to the table where Drake was sitting and sat down beside him.

Drake gave him just the barest glance and nod. No one would have noticed the reaction if they weren't looking for it.

The Kid saw it and knew the plan was on.

Proceeding as normally as possible until the time came to make their move, The Kid grabbed one of the wooden bowls and dipped it into the pot of oatmeal. As he started to eat with his fingers, he heard a stir go through the other prisoners and glanced up, expecting to see Otto getting to his feet and starting to pitch a ruckus.

Instead a shock went through him as he recognized Jillian Fletcher coming toward him, flanked by a couple guards.

"What the hell?" Drake exclaimed under his breath.

"I don't know," The Kid whispered, barely moving his lips. "Just take it easy."

"I will . . . but I don't know about Otto."

The Kid knew what Drake meant. Otto was too simple-minded to be able to count on him adjusting to new developments, like Jillian's unexpected appearance. He might well carry on as planned, despite the young woman's presence.

One thing you could say for the surprise: all the guards were looking at Jillian and not paying close attention to the prisoners.

Because of that, Drake was able to put his hand on the bench between him and The Kid for a second. When he took it away, the key to the leg irons lay there. The Kid covered it up immediately with his own hand.

"Mine are loose already," Drake whispered. "Unlock yours."

Trying to keep his movements as unobtrusive as possible, The Kid drew his legs up and reached down quickly, like he was just scratching his calf or something. With the deft touch that enabled him to be a skillful gun-handler, he found the keyhole by feel, thrust the key in, and turned it in a matter of seconds.

The leg irons clicked open around his left ankle.

That was all he managed to do before Jillian arrived at the table and looked at him. "Mr. Bledsoe," she said. "I want to talk to you about—"

At that moment, Otto let out a roar, surged to his feet, grabbed the still half-full pot of hot oatmeal from the table, and smashed it over the head of the nearest guard.

The guard collapsed. Otto grabbed his rifle but didn't try to fire it. Instead he grasped it by the barrel and used it as a club as he waded into the other guards.

Instantly, the area around the front tables was a confused melee as other prisoners joined in the fight and more guards rushed in from all over the tunnel.

But not the ones guarding the chimney, or the men who had accompanied Jillian Fletcher into Hades.

Drake took care of those two. He sprang up from the bench, holding the leg irons he had unlocked from both ankles earlier. He swung the heavy chain and irons like a mace. They crunched into the back of one guard's skull, unhinging his knees.

In a continuation of the same movement, Drake whirled and slashed the irons across the face of the other guard. Blood spurted as the makeshift weapon pulped the man's nose and opened up a huge gash in his cheek. He went down, stunned.

"Grab the girl!" Drake snapped at The Kid. "They can't shoot at us as long as we have her!"

The Kid knew Drake was right. Having Jillian as a hostage would give them an edge they hadn't even talked about. Neither of them could have predicted that she would show up, in Hades of all places, just as they were about to make their break.

The problem was that every instinct in The Kid rebelled at the idea of placing an innocent young woman in such danger. When he hesitated, Drake dropped the leg irons and lunged at Jillian. She was standing there, mouth gaping open in shock at the violence that had broken out around her.

Drake wrapped one arm around Jillian's waist

and clamped his other hand over her mouth so she couldn't scream and alert the men rushing to break up the fight that something else was going on. As he dragged her toward the rear wall of the tunnel, he called over his shoulder to The Kid, "Come on!"

The Kid jerked the unlocked leg iron from his ankle, scooped up the irons Drake had dropped, and ran after them. He didn't like what was happening, but he knew he was closer to getting out of Hell Gate than he had been since he got there. Maybe he could convince Drake to let Jillian go once they'd gotten past the guards at the chimney.

Those two men saw them coming, but they couldn't shoot with the warden's daughter in the line of fire. Drake had Jillian clutched in front of him, using her as a human shield. Her feet weren't on the ground anymore. She struggled but couldn't free herself from Drake's powerful grip.

The guards started to yell for help, but with the uproar going on at the front of the tunnel, the others couldn't hear them. The Kid sprang forward, swinging the leg irons. One of the men tried to block them with his rifle, but the irons struck his arm instead. The Kid heard bone snap.

With a hard push, The Kid shoved the injured man into the other guard and both of them went down. A swift kick to the head stretched the other guard out and silenced him.

"Damn good work!" Drake said. "I knew you'd be a fighter, Kid. Now grab one of those rifles and head on up the chimney."

"Let the girl go," The Kid said.

Drake shook his head. "When we get to the top. If they know she's with us, they won't dare fire up the chimney at us."

Drake was right, of course, The Kid picked up one of the Winchesters dropped by the guards he had overpowered and slid into the crack in the rock. As Drake had explained, it was hard to see until you were right at the opening.

The crack in the earth ran upward at a sharp angle. The Kid had to wedge his shoulders into it. He started to climb, bracing himself between the stone walls. Morning sunlight shining into the opening at the top filtered down and lit the way for him.

He made it to the turn and worked his way around it. The chimney ran almost straight up and down from there, with only a slight angle to it. He had his shoulders and back pressed to one wall, his feet to the other, and inched his way upward.

He glanced down and saw Jillian's terrified, tear-streaked face as she pulled herself around the bend in the chimney. Fear had silenced her. Drake had to be right behind her.

The Kid knew Jillian had heard Drake say they would let her go when they got to the top and took care of the guards. She was playing along, hoping he'd been telling the truth.

So did The Kid. He didn't think they needed to be saddled with a hostage, even if she was Fletcher's daughter.

The air was thick with smoke from the torches below. The acrid tang bit at The Kid's nose. He ignored it and kept climbing. He had covered half of the eighty feet above him—forty feet more to the top.

The guards on duty atop the cliff might have heard the commotion in Hades, or they might not be aware that anything was going on. Most likely they probably weren't expecting an armed, escaping prisoner to clamber out of the narrow hole. The Kid knew taking them by surprise was really the only chance he had.

When he was only about five feet from the opening, Jillian screamed.

The Kid cursed. Getting his feet under him on what had become a mostly moderate slope, he scrambled upward as fast as he could go.

The light was suddenly blocked off as one of the guards leaned over the opening and thrust the barrel of his rifle through it. The Kid found himself looking down that barrel and knew the spooked guard might start shooting at any second.

Chapter 17

Instinct and superb reflexes, despite his long confinement, allowed The Kid to fire first. The sharp crack of the rifle in his hands was deafening in the narrow confines of the chimney.

The guard jerked back out of sight. The Kid levered another round into the Winchester's chamber and clawed his way to the surface.

As he emerged from the hole in the top of the cliff, he threw himself onto his belly. A shot blasted at that instant, the bullet whipping over his head, missing him by no more than six inches.

Lying on his belly, he triggered a round at the second guard. The .44-40 slug ripped through the man's thigh and knocked him off his feet. His rifle went flying.

The Kid jerked his head from side to side, looking for the other man. Relief went through him as he spotted the man lying on the ground a few yards away, clutching a bullet-shattered shoulder and whimpering in pain.

The Kid felt an unexpected pang of sympathy as he recognized the man as Smithson, the guard who hadn't actually befriended him but had treated him with more respect than some of the others. He was glad his shot hadn't killed Smithson.

Sympathy didn't stop him from leaping to his feet and kicking both rifles away from the men who had dropped them. He swung the Winchester in his hands back and forth to cover both wounded guards.

"It's clear!" he called down to Drake.

"Get on up there, you bitch!" Drake ordered Jillian Fletcher. Sobbing, she emerged from the hole, followed closely by Drake.

The first thing he did was snatch up one of the rifles. Now that Drake was armed, too, The Kid thought it would be safe for him to take a second to look around at their surroundings.

The mouth of the natural chimney had a cluster of small boulders around it. The heavily wooded slope of a mountain rose to his left. The Kid thought that was west. To his right, about fifteen feet away, was the sheer drop-off of the cliff, running north and south farther than the eye could see.

That was why it took so long for guards to get up there, The Kid realized. They had to ride a long way to get to a trail that led to the top of the cliff.

The pair of saddled horses Smithson and the other guard had ridden to the top were tied to small trees nearby. The Kid was mighty glad to see them. Those horses represented freedom.

"Come on, Drake," he said. "Let's get out of here."

"In a minute," Drake snapped. "We've got time." He turned to Jillian and caught hold of her arm, squeezing it cruelly. "You bitch," he said again. "I told you what'd happen to you if you let out a peep while we were climbing up here."

From the ground, the guard who'd been wounded in the leg by The Kid said, "Let her go, Drake. You're out. You don't need a hostage anymore."

"The hell I don't," Drake replied with a sneer. "Fortune dropped the warden's daughter right in my lap. You reckon I'm gonna turn down that gift?"

"You said you'd let her go," The Kid reminded him.

"Well, I changed my mind. Just for playing that little trick she did, she's coming with us." Drake shoved Jillian at The Kid with such force he had to grab hold of her to keep her from falling. "Get her on one of those horses and climb up behind her. I'll finish up here."

The Kid was about to ask him what the hell he meant by that, when Drake swung up the rifle he held and fired, driving a slug into the forehead of the guard with the wounded leg. Jillian screamed as the man's head jerked back and seemed to balloon for a second before blood and brain matter exploded out of it.

With his hands full of Jillian, The Kid couldn't stop Drake before the man worked the rifle's lever and blasted another shot through Smithson's skull, killing him as well.

"What the hell do you think you're doing?" The Kid shouted.

"Making sure there's nobody to tell them which way we went," Drake answered coolly. "As well as getting a little payback for the way I was treated down here in Hades. Don't lose any sleep over those guards, Kid. Fletcher's Satan, and the guards are his little imps. They had it coming."

The Kid didn't believe that, but the men were already dead and there was nothing he could do for them.

Drake went on, "I told you to get that girl on a horse. Unless you'd rather me do it—"

Jillian cried out and cringed against The Kid. She might be afraid of him, but she was mortally terrified of Drake.

"Come on," The Kid muttered as he turned toward the horses. He kept a hand around her arm to make sure she didn't get away.

Even though it sickened him to admit it, he knew Drake was right about one thing: having Jillian with them would make their pursuers a lot more cautious and less eager to start shooting. He told himself he would keep her safe for the time being, and they could release her later.

A glance behind them revealed that Drake was busy rolling boulders over the opening to block any of the guards from climbing up after them. It must have been discovered that they had escaped.

As he and Jillian reached the horses, he told her in a low voice, "Just cooperate for now. I won't let him hurt you."

"You . . . you can't stop him," she replied in a choked voice. "He's a monster!"

The Kid couldn't deny that, not after he'd seen Drake cold-bloodedly execute both guards. "We'll get away from him," The Kid promised. "There's no reason we have to stay together." He had agreed to help Drake escape, but now they were quits. They didn't owe anything to each other anymore.

Of course, Drake might not see it that way, especially where Jillian was concerned.

The Kid would deal with that when the time came. He wanted to put as much distance between him and Hell Gate Prison as he could. He urged Jillian to climb up on one of the horses, jerked the animal's reins loose, and swung up behind her.

Drake untied the other horse and mounted it. "Let's go," he said, kicking the horse into motion and heading up the slope.

The Kid followed.

There was nothing else to do.

Drake seemed to know his way around those mountains. When The Kid asked him about that when they paused to rest the horses an hour or so later, the outlaw explained, "I spent some time in these parts a few years ago, before they ever started building that damn prison." Drake chuckled. "I was running from the law then, too."

"I haven't seen anybody behind us," The Kid commented.

"Oh, they're back there," Drake said. "It's hard to follow a trail in country this rugged, but it's not impossible. Some of those guards Fletcher has working for him are supposed to be pretty good trackers."

"We need to shake them off."

"We will, don't worry. I know some trails that not many others do, if you get my drift."

"Owlhoot trails, you mean."

Drake grinned. "Don't sound so damn superior. You're every bit as much an outlaw as I am now, Kid."

The Kid glanced over at Jillian Fletcher. She was sitting on a log, her face pale and tear-streaked but composed. She wasn't crying anymore.

He nodded toward her and said, "You could tell her I'm not Bledsoe. She already halfway believes it."

Drake laughed. "What difference would that make? You think you could turn around and go back now? You'd put your life in that madman's hands with nothing more to back up your story than the word of an escaped prisoner and a hysterical girl you kidnapped? Who just happens to be the warden's daughter, I might add."

Jillian looked up from the log. "You're really *not* Ben Bledsoe?" she asked The Kid.

"That's right," Drake said. "He's not. He's some gunfighter called Kid Morgan who just happens to look a lot like Bledsoe. He tried to tell that to your pa, but high-and-mighty Warden Fletcher wouldn't believe him."

"I . . . I wondered . . ."

"That's the reason I had to break out," The Kid said grimly. "The only way to prove I'm not Bledsoe is to find the real one and bring him back. Maybe then I can get on with my life."

And what a bitter life it was, The Kid reminded himself. Drifting in and out of trouble, mourning his murdered wife, tormenting himself with memories.

"I'm sorry," Jillian whispered. "You mean my father . . . did what he did to you . . . for nothing?"

"Are you talking about the way he whipped me within an inch of my life?" It was a harsh thing to say. He saw Jillian wince a little at his words. He softened his tone slightly as he went on, "I couldn't tell him what he wanted to know. I don't have any idea where Bledsoe's loot is cached. He's going to have to ask the real Bledsoe if he wants to find out about that."

Jillian looked down at the ground and didn't say anything after that.

They moved on a short time later. Drake proved

to be right about knowing the lonely trails. He led them through narrow gashes with rock walls rising more than a hundred feet on either side of them. He took them across rock bridges that spanned dizzying chasms and made The Kid glad the horses were surefooted. Brush-choked ravines that appeared to be impassable had paths through them after all, and Drake knew where to find them.

It was a zigzagging course. By late afternoon, The Kid estimated they had ridden a good thirty miles, but Hell Gate probably wasn't more than ten or fifteen miles behind them in a straight line.

The Kid's belly was empty. He wouldn't have thought he would miss that greasy stew so much. He hadn't gotten breakfast that morning, he reminded himself.

There were plenty of creeks in the mountains, so they wouldn't go thirsty, but the lack of supplies might prove to be a problem. "We have to find something to eat," he told Drake. "Maybe we could trap a rabbit or something."

They had spotted deer and other wild game during the day but didn't want to risk a shot or a fire to cook anything they might bring down.

"Don't worry," Drake said. "You ought to know by now, Kid, that I've always got a plan."

"Well, if you do, I'd like to know what it is."

"I haven't been just leading us around these mountains at random. I had a destination in mind as soon as we left Hell Gate." Drake pointed to the shoulder of a mountain rising above them. "There's a cabin in a little valley about a mile from here where gents in my line of work stop over from time to time."

"You're talking about a hideout."

Drake shrugged. "Call it what you want. Fellas who use it leave some supplies there if they can. There'll be jerky, canned peaches, things like that that'll keep. No lawman knows about it. The girl's pa sure as hell doesn't. We can spend the night there safely."

"All right," The Kid said with a nod. "That sounds pretty good." And in the morning, they could go their separate ways, he added to himself.

They rode on with Drake continuing to lead the way. Dusk was settling down over the rugged peaks around them when they topped a little rise and looked down into the narrow valley Drake had mentioned.

The Kid could barely make out the cabin. It was tucked into a stand of trees and blended in with them. He could believe that no lawman knew about the hideout in that high, lonesome country.

But somebody sure did, he realized, because a thin thread of gray smoke rose from the stone chimney, almost but not quite completely blending in with the graying sky.

There were horses in the pole corral built onto the side of the cabin. The Kid saw them moving around a little.

Drake could see everything that The Kid did. He said softly, "Well, well. Looks like we're gonna have to share."

And then he looked pointedly over at Jillian Fletcher.

Chapter 18

Jillian saw the look and shrank back against The Kid, her face going taut with fear.

"Forget it," The Kid said. "We'll find some other place to hole up."

"There isn't any other place, at least not around here." Drake shook his head. "Take it easy, Kid. I know what I'm doing. The girl's going to be a distraction, that's all."

"What are you talking about?"

"There are four or five horses in that corral. I don't know about you, but I don't like two-to-one odds. We're going to have to have some sort of advantage." Drake nodded toward Jillian. "She's it."

"You . . . you're going to . . . trade me to them?" she asked in a quavering voice.

Drake grunted. "Not exactly. Morgan, tear her dress so they can get a good look at one shoulder."

"What?"

"I'd do it myself, but you'd probably take offense and start a ruckus," Drake observed with a note of exasperation in his voice. "We want those old boys in that cabin looking at Miss Fletcher, not at us. That way we can get the drop on them. We'll tie them up for the night, then in the morning we can take their guns and some of their supplies and leave them with just a couple horses so they'll have to ride double. That way they can't come after us."

Now that Drake had explained, the plan sounded workable. The Kid didn't like the fact that it would put Jillian in danger, but he didn't see any way around it. Jillian would remain in danger until they got to the point where they could split up. Then he would see to it that she was left somewhere safe, like on the outskirts of a settlement.

"All right, but she can do the tearing herself," he said. "Is that all right with you, Miss Fletcher?"

"You want me to . . . tear my clothes?"

"Sorry," The Kid told her. "Like Drake said, it'll help us get the drop on those men without a lot of shooting and killing."

Jillian thought about it for a second before sighing and nodding. "All right," she said as she reached up to the collar of her dress. "If you think it's best."

She tugged on the fabric, but it proved stubborn enough that in the end, The Kid had to help her rip it so the dress hung loose from a bared shoulder.

"How's that?" he asked Drake.

The man shrugged. "Might be better if a little more skin was showing, but I reckon it'll do. Here's how we'll handle it. You'll walk down there and stop outside the cabin, miss. Morgan and I will circle around and get on either side of it. You yell for help, and when those men look out and see you standing there, they'll come out to see what's going on. Then Morgan and I will throw down on them and make them drop their guns."

"You're trusting me not to run away?"

Drake gave her a wolfish grin in the fading light. "Where are you gonna run to? We're miles from the prison and farther than that from any town. There's nobody up in these mountains except panthers and bears and outlaws, and night's coming on. You wouldn't make it until morning, Miss Fletcher." He nodded toward The Kid. "Your best bet to stay alive is to cooperate with us."

"All right," she said in a small voice. "I'll do it."

"Now you're being smart. Give us about five minutes to get in position. Kid, you take the left, I'll take the right. There are enough trees all around that cabin to let us get pretty close."

The Kid nodded. "I understand."

He stayed in the saddle and helped Jillian down from the horse. When she looked up at him worriedly, he told her, "You'll be fine."

"Just don't think about trying to double-cross us," Drake warned. "I promise you, you'd be a whole hell of a lot worse off with those hombres than you are with us."

Jillian gave The Kid an intent look and said, "I know."

She was counting on him to protect her. He hadn't wanted that responsibility, but now that it had been thrust upon him, he couldn't ignore it. Rebel's death had hardened him inside, left a cold spot in his heart that might never warm again, but still, he was Frank Morgan's son. There were some things he just couldn't dodge.

"Let's go," Drake said. "We don't want to lose all the light. Don't make any more noise than you have to, Morgan."

The Kid nodded and turned his horse. He moved off to the left along the rise and began angling down into the valley on a course that would take him to the side of the cabin.

He wanted to look back at Jillian, but he didn't. She had a part to play in this game, too, and she would have to play it well for any of them to survive.

The Kid concentrated on approaching the cabin stealthily. He dismounted when he was still a good hundred yards away and moved closer on foot after tying the horse's reins to a sapling. He stopped behind a thick-trunked pine about twenty feet from the front corner of the cabin.

The daylight continued to fade, but enough remained that he could see Jillian making her way down the hill. She moved quickly, stumbling a little when she glanced back over her shoulder as if afraid someone was after her.

The Kid smiled faintly in admiration. The young woman had sand, no doubt about that, and she was smart. If one of the owlhoots in the cabin spotted her, he would think she was running away from somebody.

Her bare shoulder gleamed in the dusk as she came panting to a halt in front of the cabin, a good fifty feet from the door.

"Hello!" she cried. "Is anybody in there? If there is, you have to help me! Please, help me!"

In his life as Conrad Browning, The Kid had seen a number of stage plays starring famous actresses. None of them had ever given a better performance than the one Jillian Fletcher gave, for an audience of outlaws using a hideout in some isolated New Mexico mountains. She sounded absolutely terrified.

Probably because she was, The Kid thought.

The Kid saw the cabin door swing open. A scruffy-looking man in range clothes stepped out, gun in hand. A ginger-colored beard jutted from his chin.

"Oh, thank God!" Jillian exclaimed as she took a step toward him. "You heard me!"

The man swung his gun up and snapped, "Hold it right there, miss! Who are you? What in blazes are you doin' out here in the middle o' nowhere?"

Jillian stopped and held her hands out imploring. "You have to help me. I-I'm lost. My horse threw me, and I've been wandering in the woods for hours, and I-I think something was chasing me! It sounded like . . . like a bear!"

"You're alone?" the ginger-bearded outlaw asked, his voice still edged with suspicion.

"Of course. I got separated from the rest of my party. They were hunting, and . . . and I don't know where they are . . ."

She was improvising, The Kid knew, but she was doing a good job of it.

The man chuckled. "Some rich folks out on a huntin' expedition, eh?"

"That's right," Jillian agreed.

The Kid heard the greed in the outlaw's voice as the man went on, "I'll bet your friends are mighty worried about you. They'd probably pay a pretty penny to get you back safe and sound."

"That's right! I'm sure there would be a reward."

It wouldn't be a reward, thought The Kid. It would be ransom. And Jillian likely wouldn't be returned all that safe and sound. There was no telling what sort of indignities she would have to endure at the hands of that bunch, even if they did decide to keep her alive and try to cash in on that.

His hands tightened on the rifle he held. As soon as all the men came out of the cabin, they would find that *they* were the prisoners, not Jillian.

The corral was on The Kid's side of the cabin. He was close enough to get an accurate count of the horses inside it. There were four mounts, four saddles hanging on the fence. Three men were still inside the cabin.

"Come on out, fellas," the bearded outlaw called as he lowered his gun. He had obviously decided Jillian didn't represent a threat. "Look what Lady Luck done dropped right in our laps."

He walked closer to her. She retreated a step, saying, "You . . . you won't hurt me, will you?"

"Hurt you?" the man repeated. "Aw, honey, we wouldn't never hurt a pretty little gal like you. We're gonna take real good care o' you until we can get you back to your folks." Leering, he looked back over his shoulder at his three companions, who had come out of the cabin. "Ain't that right, fellas?"

The three men crowded up behind him, clearly eager to get a better look at Jillian. Their guns were holstered, and as the four of them approached her, the first man pouched his iron, too.

The Kid knew he wouldn't get a better chance. He stepped out from behind the tree, leveled his rifle at the four outlaws, and called, "Hold it! Drop your guns!"

They spun toward the sound of his voice, hands clawing at their holstered revolvers. The Kid expected them to freeze once they saw that he had the drop on them, but if they didn't, he would open fire and Drake would, too.

Drake didn't wait. A rifle cracked on the other side of the cabin, and one of the outlaws pitched forward as a .44-40 slug smashed into his back.

The Kid muttered a curse. They had been so close to ending it without any gunplay, but there was no longer any chance of that. Drake's shot had started the ball, and there was no calling it back.

The Kid's sights were leveled on the chest of the ginger-bearded outlaw. He squeezed the trigger and felt the Winchester's butt kick against his shoulder as the rifle cracked.

The owlhoot's gun was halfway out of its holster, but he dropped it as he staggered back a step and pawed at the hole where The Kid's bullet had driven deep into his chest.

Swinging the rifle toward the two men who were still threats, The Kid jacked the lever and fired again. From the corner of his eye, he saw that Jillian had spun around and was running away, getting out of the line of fire. That was good, he thought as he levered and fired a third round, then a fourth.

From the other side of the cabin, Drake's weapon continued to roar, too.

Acrid powdersmoke stung The Kid's nose as he stopped firing and lowered the rifle a little to peer over the barrel. All four of the outlaws were on the ground, lying motionless. A couple of them had guns in their hands, and he had been vaguely aware during the fight that they had gotten off a few shots.

None of the bullets had come close to him. He hoped the same was true of Drake and especially Jillian.

He looked toward the spot where she had been. He saw her figure disappearing into the shadows gathering on the hillside that overlooked the cabin.

"She's getting away!" Drake shouted as he ran out into the open. "Go get her, Kid!"

Drake was covering the four owlhoots in case any of them were still alive. The Kid broke into a run, his long legs carrying him across the clearing in front of the cabin and up the slope after Jillian.

Chapter 19

In the fading light, The Kid followed Jillian as much by sound as by sight. He could hear her crashing through the brush ahead of him.

"Miss Fletcher!" he called. "Jillian! Stop! It's all right!"

She kept going. He supposed after everything she had been through, the terrible crash of gun-thunder had been too much for her. She was running blindly, trying to get away from her fear.

He caught up with her before she reached the top of the rise. With a lunge, he wrapped his free arm around her waist and hauled her to a stop.

She fought him, twisting in his grip and crying, "No! Leave me alone! Leave me alone!"

"Miss Fletcher, stop!" he said in an attempt to cut through her panic. "It's me, Kid Morgan."

She continued struggling for a moment, then her efforts to get away began to subside. Her eyes were still wild as she looked up at him, but comprehension had begun to creep back into them.

"Mr. Morgan?" she whispered.

"Yes, it's me," The Kid told her. "You're all right. The shooting is over. Nothing's going to happen to you."

She sagged against him, her muscles going limp. Her head rested on his chest. He felt the rapid beating of her heart, like that of a bird held captive in the hand.

"I thought . . . I thought I was going to die," she murmured. "All that shooting . . ."

"You were out of the line of fire, for the most part. But you did good to get farther away. We need to go back now."

"I thought you were going to . . . going to take those men prisoner."

"So did I," The Kid said.

Carl Drake had had a different idea. Drake hadn't given the outlaws a chance to surrender. He had opened up on them as soon as they reacted to The Kid's voice.

To be fair, they had been reaching for their guns when Drake started shooting. Given the way they had been looking at Jillian before the trouble started, The Kid wasn't going to lose any sleep over their deaths. Given the chance, they would have gleefully taken turns assaulting her.

The Kid steered her down the slope. "Let's go," he said. "According to Drake, there'll be food in the cabin."

"I couldn't eat," Jillian murmured. "Not after everything I've seen today."

"You have to," The Kid told her. "You need to keep your strength up."

"Why? It would be simpler to just starve to death."

"You feel like that now. People can go through a lot, though, and deep down, they still want to live."

He was proof of that. Despite everything he had lost, no matter how often he thought about how much easier it would be to let go and join Rebel in death, when the time came to fight, he fought for his life, again and again. He thought about that and realized maybe he *did* have something left to live for, after all. Even if he wasn't exactly sure what it was.

By the time they got back to the cabin, Drake had dragged the carcasses into a row and stripped them of their gunbelts, which he had looped over his shoulder. He grinned at The Kid and Jillian and said, "Good. You found her."

Jillian shuddered and looked away from the bloody corpses.

The Kid said, "I thought we were going to tie them up and leave some supplies and a couple horses in the morning."

Drake shrugged. "They wanted to make a fight of it. I figured it'd be better if we obliged them."

The Kid couldn't argue with that, although he suspected Drake probably had intended to kill the men all along, if he got half a chance. It certainly simplified matters.

"Go on inside," Drake went on, nodding

toward the cabin. "There's coffee on the stove and beans and salt pork cooking as well. We'll eat good tonight, Kid. Better than we have in a long time."

That fact was beyond dispute. And it would do Jillian good to get away from the bodies.

"What are you going to do with them?" The Kid asked quietly.

"There's a ravine over yonder a little ways," Drake replied. "Looks like I can dump them in it and then cave in the bank on top of them. That's the closest we're gonna come to being able to bury them."

"It'll have to do," The Kid agreed with a nod as he ushered Jillian toward the door. "You need any help?"

"No, I'll take care of it. You keep an eye on Miss Fletcher."

That would also give Drake a chance to finish going through the dead men's pockets, The Kid thought. He didn't begrudge Drake anything he found. The Kid wasn't interested in money, only in clearing his name.

"Take a look around in there and see if you can find any clothes that'll fit us," Drake called after them as The Kid and Jillian went inside. "I'd like to get rid of these prison duds."

The Kid agreed with that sentiment wholeheartedly. As he closed the door, he saw that Drake was already pulling the boots off the feet of the dead outlaws.

The smell of the Arbuckle's brewing, along

with the aroma of beans and pork, made The Kid's mouth water. Jillian still insisted she didn't want anything, but when he found a reasonably clean tin cup and poured some coffee in it, she took it and sipped from it gratefully.

Two Winchesters, an old Henry rifle, and a heavy caliber Sharps carbine leaned in a corner. The Sharps was much like the rifle that Phillip Bearpaw had given The Kid more than a year earlier. It seemed like a lifetime ago, and he knew he would probably never see that particular weapon again. It was long gone, along with his horse, his Colt, and all his other gear.

But as long as a man was still alive, he could start over, and that was what The Kid intended to do. He poured a cup of coffee for himself and sipped it as he began going through the saddlebags stacked on the rough-hewn table that was the biggest piece of furniture in the single-room cabin.

In addition to the table and the wood-burning stove, there were a couple chairs, a crate and an empty keg that could also serve as seats, and four crude bunks, one on each wall. There was certainly nothing fancy about the place, but an owl-hoot on the run from the law wouldn't care about fancy.

The Kid found several spare shirts in the out-laws' gear that looked like they would fit him and Drake, as well as a pair of denim trousers for each of them. As Drake had predicted, there was also a good stock of provisions on hand. It would keep them going for a while.

Drake came in a short time later carrying the boots and hats he had taken from the dead men. He dumped the boots on the floor and the hats on the table.

"Take your pick, Kid," he said. "It'll be good to dress like a normal hombre again, instead of a prisoner."

"Amen to that," The Kid muttered. He picked up one of the hats, a pearl gray Stetson, and checked the inside of it for anything crawling before he put it on. As he settled it on his head, he asked Jillian, "How's that look?"

She mustered up a weak smile. "Very dashing," she said.

Drake chose a dark brown hat with a concho-studded band. Jillian turned her back while the two men went through the clothes and picked out and tried on what they wanted.

The Kid settled for a faded blue bib-front shirt. The jeans were a little short, but they would do. He found a pair of black, high-topped boots that fit fairly well, and tucked the trouser legs down in them—nobody could tell they were short.

One of the gunbelts Drake had brought in fit well enough. Having the weight of a sturdy Colt revolver on his hip made The Kid feel better than he had in weeks.

He supposed it was a sad commentary on a man's life when he had to be packing a shooting iron in order to feel fully dressed, but there it was. He grasped the gun butt and moved the weapon up and down in the leather. It drew smooth and didn't catch on anything.

Drake pulled on a flannel shirt and a brown vest. One of the outlaws had preferred a cross-draw rig, and Drake chose it to buckle around his waist. The holstered Colt rode on his left hip, butt forward. Men who had mastered that draw were usually very fast and slick with it, but The Kid liked a more traditional draw.

By the time they were outfitted, it was fully dark outside. The room was lit by a couple stubby candles set in tin plates on the table.

The Kid checked the beans and salt pork, found they were done, and dished up bowls for all three of them. Jillian picked at her food but finally wound up eating most of what he gave her. He and Drake tore into the food with good appetites. They washed it down with swigs of the hot, black coffee.

"I'm sorry about the way you were treated, Mr. Morgan," Jillian said. "I'm sure my father really believed you were that man Bledsoe, or he . . . he wouldn't have done the things he did. You really do bear an amazing resemblance to him, you know."

"The lady's right, Kid," Drake said with a grin. "You do."

"Well, it would have been fine with me if I'd gone my whole life without discovering that," The Kid said.

Drake shrugged. "Trouble usually seeks out folks whether they're looking for it or not."

The Kid changed the subject by suggesting, "We'd better take turns standing watch tonight."

"I'm not going to try to get away, if that's what you're worried about," Jillian said. "I know I couldn't survive up here in the mountains by myself, especially not at night."

The Kid shook his head. "That's not what I was thinking of. If Carl knew about this cabin, it stands to reason that other men do, too. We don't want to be surprised like the, ah, previous occupants were."

"You mean other outlaws," Drake said, chuckling. "You're right. Somebody could show up expecting to make themselves at home. We ought to be ready if they do."

Jillian looked down at her plate and bit her lip. She understood what they were talking about, The Kid thought. If another bunch of desperadoes rode in and saw her, chances were they would try to kill him and Drake and take Jillian for themselves.

"You can have whichever watch you want," he told Drake.

"I'll take the first one. I reckon I'm still a mite stronger than you, Kid, so you need some sleep first. I'll wake you an hour or two after midnight."

The Kid nodded. "All right."

He was a little leery about going to sleep and trusting that Drake wouldn't double-cross him, but he didn't have much choice in the matter. Already, exhaustion was trying to claim him.

Anyway, if Drake wanted to shoot him in the back, he'd had plenty of chances to do so. Since The Kid had seen ample evidence of how ruthless Drake could be, he had no doubt Drake would have done just that, if such had been his intention.

"Tomorrow morning, we can pack up some of these supplies and head out," The Kid went on. "We'll be going our separate ways."

Drake surprised him by shaking his head. "Not hardly," the man said.

"What do you mean?" The Kid asked with a frown.

"We're sticking together, Kid," Drake declared.

"There's no need for that. We agreed that we'd help each other escape, but now that we're out, I'm going to track down Bledsoe and prove that I'm not him."

"Exactly. And I can give you a hand with that, because . . . well, it just so happens, I know where Bledsoe was going when he busted out of Hell Gate."

Chapter 20

The Kid stared across the rough table at Drake. "You never said anything about that before, back in Hades," he said.

Drake shrugged again. "You never played your cards close to your vest, Morgan? I wanted out of that place, and if I'd spilled everything I know at once, you wouldn't have had any reason to let me string along with you. You could've double-crossed me . . . just like Bledsoe did."

"You didn't say anything about that, either."

"Here's the way it was." Drake clasped both hands around his coffee cup and leaned forward. "The reason I knew how Bledsoe busted out of Hell Gate was because we worked out the plan together. I found that chimney in the cliff and told him how he could use it to get out. We agreed that I'd go with him, and when he went to get that loot of his, I'd have a share of it coming to me."

"But he escaped on his own without telling you he was going," The Kid guessed.

"That's right. He promised me a payoff and then cheated me on it, because he already knew what he needed to know. No offense, Morgan, but *that's* why I didn't tell you how we were getting out until we were ready to go. I couldn't take a chance on you being a treacherous son of a bitch like Bledsoe."

"How do you know where he was going after he escaped?"

"While we were still working out all the details, he let it slip that he intended to head to . . . a certain place, let's say . . . after he picked up the money he had stashed. Said he had friends out there, including a girl he wanted to see again. He made it sound like he was going to stay for a while. He thought he'd be safe there."

The Kid regarded Drake intently. "But you're not ready to say where that certain place is, are you?"

Drake grinned and shook his head. "Hell, no. But I'll take you there."

"Because you still want that share of Bledsoe's loot."

"Nope." Drake's voice hardened as he shook his head. "Since he double-crossed me, I've decided I want all of it. All of it that's left, anyway."

"That money rightfully belongs to other people," The Kid pointed out. "The people Bledsoe stole it from in the first place."

"Yeah, other people I don't know and don't

give a damn about. Anyway, most of it came from the banks and the railroads, and nobody cares about them."

Except the people who had their money in those banks, and the ones who owned stock in the railroads, The Kid thought. But he didn't say it because he knew Drake wouldn't understand such a thing or care about it if he did.

"Why did you throw in with me?" he asked. Curiosity, along with the surprise he felt at Drake's revelations, had chased away his weariness, at least for the time being.

"I figured two men would stand a better chance of getting out of there, and once they were out, they'd be more likely to be able to settle Bledsoe's hash. Besides that, you've got an even stronger motive than I do for tracking him down. As long as *he's* free, *you're* a fugitive, too."

That was true, The Kid thought as he nodded slowly.

"So you see," Drake went on, "however much of Bledsoe's loot I can get my hands on is my price for helping you clear your name, Kid. That seems fair enough, doesn't it?"

"I suppose so," The Kid said. "I don't have much choice in the matter, do I?"

"Well, you can try to pick up Bledsoe's trail on your own, I reckon. But finding him that way might take you weeks or months or even years. You might never find him. And you'd never know when some bounty hunter or small-town lawdog might recognize you and start shooting.

I can promise you, the bounty on your head is gonna be dead or alive, Kid, dead or alive." Drake sat back and spread his hands. "Or you can play along with me, and I can take you right to where Bledsoe was headed in about a week. He's had time to recover that money by now, so chances are, that's where he'll be. Your choice, Kid . . . maybe years as a fugitive, or a week's ride to the showdown."

The Kid didn't have to think about it for very long. He nodded and said, "You've got a deal, Drake."

"Good. You won't be sorry."

"There's just one thing we have to figure out." The Kid turned his head to look at Jillian, who had been listening to the conversation between them with rapt attention. "What are we going to do with Miss Fletcher?"

"I can answer that," Jillian spoke up before Drake could say anything.

Both men frowned in surprise.

"I'm going with you," she went on.

Drake looked skeptical. "Now, I'm not sure that's such a good idea—"

"Forget it," The Kid said flatly. "The first settlement we come to, we're going to ride close enough to leave you just outside town, where you'll be safe."

"No," Jillian said. "I feel terrible about what my father did to you, Mr. Morgan. It was completely unfair. I want to make it up to you, and I'm going to do that by helping you find Bledsoe."

"No offense, but that's the craziest thing I've ever heard."

"Not at all," she insisted. "What are you going to do when you find Bledsoe?"

"Take him back to Hell Gate and force your father to admit that I'm not who he thought I was."

"That's all well and good," Jillian said, "but what if that's not possible?"

Drake rubbed his jaw in thought. "I think I see where you're going with this," he mused. "Something could've happened to Bledsoe."

"Exactly. Men die violently out here all the time. Someone could have shot him, or an animal could have attacked him. Not only that, but say he made it safely to wherever it is Mr. Drake thinks he went. He's not going to just surrender and agree to come along peacefully when you show up, Mr. Morgan."

Drake nodded. "The lady's got a point. Bledsoe could easily wind up dead once we're through with him."

"So then I'd be able to testify that I saw the two of you with my own eyes," Jillian said. "My father might not want to believe it, but he wouldn't have much choice except to do so."

"Do you really think you could convince him?" The Kid asked. "He seemed like a pretty stubborn man to me."

"I can convince him," Jillian said with a nod. "Believe me, Mr. Morgan. Your chances of clearing your name will be better if I come along . . .

and my conscience will be a little clearer, too, although I doubt if anything I do can wipe away the stain of my father's brutal actions."

The Kid shook his head. "He was the one with the whip, not you. You don't have any call to feel guilty about it."

Jillian started to look a little uncomfortable. "He might not have been quite so angry to start with if I hadn't played that trick on him. My mother really did want to see him that day, but I hung back on purpose because I knew the guards were bringing you to his office. I . . . I wanted to see you again. I was . . . curious about you."

The Kid didn't press the issue. He didn't want to embarrass her any more than she already was. "All right," he said. "Just to be clear, though, I think this is a bad idea. I still think we ought to leave you someplace safe as soon as we can."

She smiled, one of the few times he had seen that expression on her face instead of the sheer terror that had usually been there, since leaving Hell Gate.

"It'll work out for the best, Mr. Morgan. You'll see."

He heaved a sigh. "If you're going to be riding with us, maybe you'd better start calling me Kid."

"All right, I can do that."

"You can't ride all the way to wherever it is we're going dressed like that."

"One of the men you . . . I mean, one of the men who was staying here before . . . I noticed he was on the small side. I might be able to find a shirt and a pair of pants that belonged to him. They'd still be too big, but I could roll up the sleeves and the legs and maybe get by with them."

The Kid waved a hand toward the pile of clothing he'd scavenged from the dead men's saddle-bags. "Help yourself to anything you want."

"We've got six horses now," Drake pointed out. "I took the two we brought from Hell Gate into the corral with the others. That means we each have a couple mounts. We can switch back and forth and keep them fairly fresh. That'll let us move a little faster. We can get where we're going in a week. I'm sure of it."

Seven days to a showdown, The Kid thought. Seven days until he confronted the man whose resemblance to him had landed him in Hades . . . literally as well as figuratively.

In all likelihood, seven days until more of the bloodshed and death that seemed to follow him everywhere he went.

Chapter 21

The Kid slept lightly that night while Carl Drake was standing guard. He didn't fully trust Drake, although if the man was telling the truth about everything, he had no reason to double-cross The Kid. They needed each other in order to get what they both wanted.

Jillian Fletcher was the wild card. Being around a beautiful woman made it difficult for some men to act logically and in their own best interests.

So far Drake hadn't shown any signs of being interested in her as anything except a potential hostage if pursuit from the prison caught up to them, but there was always a chance he'd been hiding his true feelings.

As for The Kid, he didn't have any romantic feelings for her. Even if he had been ready to move on with that part of his life, which he wasn't, the fact that Jillian's father was such a sadistic bastard would have squelched any feelings of affection he might have toward her. The Kid wasn't going to forget that whipping anytime soon.

The night passed peacefully, although while he was awake and standing his turn on guard duty, he noticed how restless Jillian's slumber was.

She tossed and turned and made little noises as if her sleep was haunted by nightmares. It probably was, considering everything that had happened to her and all the violence she had witnessed in the past twenty-four hours.

Before dawn the next morning, he started coffee brewing and began frying up some flapjacks and bacon. The smells woke both Jillian and Drake.

When Jillian said that she needed to step outside, Drake said, "Fine, but I'm going with you."

She gave him a hard stare. "I'm not going to run off, Mr. Drake. I told you, I want to go with the both of you and help Mr. Morgan clear his name."

"Yeah, I know, but at this time of morning, there are liable to be bears or mountain lions wandering around out there. I'll give you as much privacy as I can, but you're liable to want somebody with a rifle close by."

"Oh." Jillian looked down at the split-logged floor. "I see. In that case . . . thank you."

They went outside and came back a few minutes later. The Kid hadn't heard any sort of ruckus and assumed no varmints had interrupted anything. The coffee was ready, so he poured it into tin cups from the gear of the dead outlaws.

After breakfast, The Kid and Drake went out to

look over the horses. The mounts that had belonged to the dead outlaws appeared to be good ones.

Jillian stayed in the cabin to look through the clothes and try to find something more suitable for riding. A short time later she came out dressed in jeans and a flannel shirt. The shirtsleeves were rolled up several turns, as were the trouser legs, but other than that the clothes seemed to fit fairly well.

She had donned the boots that had belonged to the smallest of the outlaws and held a battered black hat in her hands. When she piled her auburn hair on top of her head and then put the hat on, it fit fairly well.

She asked the question most women would have asked under the circumstances. "How do I look?"

Drake smiled. "Not quite like a man, but at a distance you might pass for one."

"Is that a good thing?"

The Kid said, "It is when the authorities are looking for two men and a woman. A posse would be less likely to pay attention to three men."

"Oh," Jillian said. "I understand." She paused. "Should I have a gun?"

"There'll be a rifle in your saddle boot," Drake told her. "Have you even shot a handgun?"

"Well . . . no."

"You're better off without one, then," The Kid said. "You'd be liable to shoot yourself, or one of us."

She looked a little offended at that blunt

statement, but she shrugged and nodded. "All right. When are we leaving?"

"As soon as we can pack up all the gear and supplies we're taking with us," Drake said.

That and getting the horses ready to ride took another half hour. The Kid tied the three spare mounts together and fastened the lead rope to his saddle horn.

"I'll bring up the rear with the extra horses," he said as he swung up into the saddle. "Drake, you take the lead, since you know where we're going. Miss Fletcher, you can ride between us. That'll be the safest spot for you."

She summoned up a smile. "You told me to call you Kid," she said. "If I'm going to do that, you have to call me Jillian."

He didn't know if she was flirting with him or just trying to be friendly. Either way, he didn't see any need to be rude to her, so he nodded and said, "All right, Jillian. You need any help getting up there?"

She shook her head and said, "No, I've ridden before. Not astride, mind you, but it can't be that hard."

She grasped the horn, put her foot in the stirrup, and lifted herself, swinging her other leg over the horse's back. A cry of alarm escaped from her as she leaned too far and almost toppled off the other side of the horse. Only a desperate clutch of the saddle horn prevented the fall.

As she straightened in the saddle, she said

quickly, "I'm all right, I'm all right. I'll get the hang of it, I promise."

The Kid managed not to chuckle. He saw Drake hiding a grin as well.

"I'm sure you will," The Kid said. "It just takes some getting used to, is all."

He knew by the time the sun set again, after a day in the saddle, Jillian's muscles would be sore as hell. He could do nothing about that. It was her choice to continue along with them, after all. She wasn't really a prisoner anymore. From a practical standpoint, staying with the two men was the smart thing for her to do.

They set out, Drake leading the way along a twisting path that serpentined its way up the mountain. The landscape around them was wild and lonely, which came as no surprise to The Kid. Men who rode the owlhoot trails spent a lot of their time as far from civilization as possible.

The day was as long and hard on Jillian as The Kid had worried it would be. She didn't make any complaint, but every time they called a halt to rest the horses, he saw the way she bit her lip to stifle a groan of pain as she dismounted. Her face was pale and drawn.

They switched horses at midday, ate a cold meal of flapjacks and bacon left over from breakfast, and moved on. It was impossible to travel very fast in those rugged mountains. By the time they made camp that night, The Kid estimated that they had gone less than twenty miles.

But it was that many more miles between him

and Hell Gate Prison, he told himself. The best thing about the day was that they hadn't seen any signs of pursuit. It would be pushing their luck to think they had already given the slip to the search parties Fletcher must have sent after them, but that appeared to be the case.

After everything that had happened during the past few weeks, he would take all the luck he could get, however improbable.

Drake had found a secluded glade high on the shoulder of a mountain, not far below a pass. He reined in and said, "This is as good a place as any, I reckon."

Jillian couldn't hold back her reaction when she swung down from her horse. "Ohhhh," she said as she slumped against the animal and clung to the stirrup to keep from collapsing as her legs tried to fold up beneath her.

The Kid had already dismounted. Quickly, he stepped over to her and grasped her arm to steady her.

"It'll get better," he assured her.

"When?" she gasped. "I didn't know it was possible to hurt this much."

"Well, it'll take a few days," The Kid admitted.

"Is there anything that will help it?"

"Maybe some liniment, if we had any . . . which we don't."

And if they'd had somebody to apply it, he thought. He certainly wasn't going to rub liniment into the sore muscles of Jillian Fletcher's bare inner thighs. That would have been just asking for trouble. So in a way it was a good thing those outlaws hadn't had any liniment among their supplies.

They had had several bottles of whiskey, though, one of which Drake now pulled out of a saddlebag.

"A dollop of this in your coffee tonight will make you feel a little better," he told Jillian.

"I'll take it," she muttered as she let go of the horse and with The Kid's help tottered over to a large, flat rock, where she sat down. "I'd like to help make camp, but I don't think I can right now. I'm not sure I can even move again."

"Don't worry about it," The Kid said.

"Yes, but I don't want you to think I'm not pulling my weight."

"Just help me clear my name," he said. "That's all I want from you, Jillian."

He turned away to unsaddle his horse. As he did, he saw something flicker in her eyes. He couldn't be sure because the light was fading, but he thought it might be disappointment that he didn't want anything else from her.

The Kid and Drake took turns standing watch again that night. Jillian was restless once more, most likely from sore muscles. The whiskey in her coffee might have helped, but it couldn't make the aches go away entirely. She would hurt even worse in the morning, when those muscles had had a chance to stiffen up.

Sure enough, The Kid had to help her to her

feet when it came time to rise. She hobbled around the camp like she was a hundred years old.

"Maybe you've changed your mind about coming with us all the way to where we're going," The Kid said.

She frowned at him and shook her head. "No, I haven't. I'll be fine." She winced as she took a step. "Eventually."

"Suit yourself. The coffee will be ready in a few minutes."

A short time later, they mounted up and pushed on. Jillian insisted she didn't need any help and managed to get in the saddle by herself.

She was a tough young woman, The Kid thought. But with Jonas Fletcher as her father, it wasn't surprising. She would have to be tough to survive being raised by a man like that.

They rode through the high pass, and the view in both directions was incredible. Miles and miles of the rugged New Mexico landscape spread out before and behind them. The blue dome of the sky arched over snowcapped gray peaks and deep green valleys. The world appeared new, just born, untouched by man's violent hand.

The Kid knew how deceptive that was. Death often lurked behind the beauty. The man who let himself be lulled into believing the world was a peaceful, pristine place wouldn't live very long. Savagery went hand in hand with tranquility and could strike at any time, without warning.

Thrusting those gloomy thoughts out of his

head, he started down from the pass with his companions. "We're still heading west," he called to Drake, who rode at the head of the short column.

The man looked back and grinned. "That's right, we are. You trying to find out where we're headed, Kid?"

"Just curious, that's all."

"You'll find out soon enough," Drake promised. "You'll be face-to-face with old Bloody Ben before you know it."

That day couldn't come soon enough to suit The Kid.

The three riders and the extra horses moved through the pass. An hour later they were far enough down the mountain that they could no longer see the pass, even if they had turned around in their saddles to look.

No one was watching as a lone man on horseback, leading a pack animal, rode through the gap in the peaks and took the same westward trail.

Chapter 22

On the seventh day after escaping from Hell Gate Prison, the three riders drew rein atop a low, rocky ridge, and Carl Drake said, "There it is. Gehenna, Arizona."

The Kid rested his hands on his saddle horn and leaned forward in the leather. A few days earlier, he had finally taken the time to shave with a razor he'd found in one of the saddlebags. Now that he'd scraped off the whiskers, his face was all hard planes and angles again. His skin had been pale at first, but it was acquiring a healthy tan once more.

"Let me get this straight," he said. "We've come from Hades to Gehenna?"

Drake grinned. "That's right. Bledsoe said that was one reason he had a soft spot in his heart for this place. Said he'd lived like the devil all his life, so it was fitting that he came from a town called Gehenna."

"The place of punishment," The Kid murmured, remembering the Bible stories of his youth.

"It doesn't look like much," Jillian said from where she sat on horseback between the two men.

Gehenna wasn't impressive, that was true, even as frontier settlements went. Its only street stretched for five blocks lined with a dusty, sun-bleached mixture of buildings. Several dozen adobe dwellings were scattered haphazardly around the town's business district of frame buildings. A creek with banks dotted by scrubby mesquite trees meandered past the southern edge of the settlement.

The landscape had changed dramatically from the mountains of New Mexico where their journey had begun. The Kid figured the peaks looming in a bluish-gray line several miles to the south were in Mexico, since Gehenna wasn't far from the border.

The terrain in the area was flat except for some occasional rolling hills and long, shallow ridges like the one on which the three riders had reined to a halt. The sandy, semi-arid plains stretched as far as the eye could see to the north, east, and west.

"Why is there even a town here?" Jillian continued. "There's not a railroad or any other reason I can see for anyone to settle in such a godforsaken place."

Drake pointed to the mountains across the border. "I'm just going by what Bledsoe told me, you understand," he said, "but there are supposed to be several big ranches over there in Mexico, as well as some gold and silver mines in the mountains. This is actually the closest place for the dons who own those haciendas to get supplies, and their vaqueros come here to blow off steam. The mines are owned by Americans, and they send their ore out by mule train to Tucson. The trail comes right through here. So between the vaqueros, the mule-skinners, and the American pistoleros hired by the miners to guard those ore shipments, Gehenna is full of tough hombres. It's a wide-open town. The people who live there make most of their money off various forms of vice, if you know what I mean."

The Kid grunted and commented dryly, "Bledsoe must have talked a lot about the place."

"What else was there to do in Hades?" Drake asked with a shrug.

"So what do we do now?" Jillian asked. "Ride in and start asking people if they've seen Bledsoe?"

"That's a good plan," Drake said, "if you want to get shot in the back."

Jillian flushed. "Well, I don't know anything about tracking down an outlaw!"

The Kid glanced at the sky, which was rosy from the glow of the lowering sun barely above the horizon. "It'll be dark in a little while," he said. "Probably best to wait until then before we ride in."

"That's right," Drake agreed. "But you'll be the only one riding in, Kid. If Bledsoe spotted me, he'd recognize me right away."

"He won't recognize me? I'm the one who's supposed to look so much like him!"

"Yeah, but he doesn't know you exist, so he won't be expecting to see anybody who looks like him." Drake smiled. "He won't be on the lookout for you, so to speak. Now that you've shaved that beard off, the resemblance will be even less. If he sees you, he might think you look a little familiar, but he won't know you."

"What about me?" Jillian asked.

"He saw you at Hell Gate, didn't he?"

"Yes, I suppose so."

"He'll remember you. Men don't forget a beautiful woman."

Jillian glanced down at herself. "I'm not very beautiful now, sunburned and dressed in men's clothes and covered with trail dust!"

The things she said about her appearance were true, but The Kid could have argued with her opinion on whether or not she was beautiful. The sun had put color in her cheeks and the hard days of riding had taken some of the softness out of her features. She had gotten used to spending hours in the saddle and no longer had trouble keeping up with him and Drake. The steel core that could be found in all good frontier women was starting to show through in places.

But Drake was right about Bledsoe recognizing her. The Kid said, "There's too big a chance he might spot you. I'll go in and have a look around first. Once I've gotten the lay of the land, we can rendezvous and figure out how to proceed from there."

"All right," Jillian said with a sigh. "It sounds like this could take a while."

"It could," The Kid admitted.

"I was looking forward to a hot bath. It seems like a year since I've had one."

"You'll have to wait a while longer, I'm afraid."

"I'll be all right. Don't worry about me."

Drake said, "We'd better find a place to camp where we won't be in such easy view of the town."

The Kid pointed down the slope. "What about those trees over there by that wash?"

Drake nodded. "Yeah, it looks like there's a little bowl there where we can build a fire without it being seen."

They rode down the ridge, rocks clattering and sliding around the hooves of the horses, and a short time later came to the grove of cottonwoods next to a dry wash. No water flowed in the arroyo at the moment, but every time it rained a torrent likely rushed through, providing enough moisture for the roots of the trees to take hold.

A little grass grew, so the horses would have some graze. The Kid and Drake unsaddled and picketed the animals with some help from Jillian, who was growing more experienced in such things. She lent a hand around camp, which she hadn't been able to do starting out.

She caught a moment alone with The Kid, while Drake was working with the horses, and said quietly, "I'm a little worried about staying out here alone with Mr. Drake."

"He's treated you proper so far."

She nodded. "Yes, that's true, but you've always been close by, Kid. He wouldn't try anything as long as you're around."

The Kid thought back to the swift ruthlessness with which Drake had acted at times and said, "I wouldn't be so sure about that. I don't think he's scared of me, if that's what you mean."

"Maybe not, but he respects your abilities. That's the reason he brought you along. He thinks you can help him get what he wants from Bledsoe."

The Kid shrugged. "As long as we both get what we want, that's all right."

"I just wish I was going into town with you."

"Maybe you can, in a day or two. I'll have to see if Bledsoe is still in these parts first, and if he is, where he spends most of his time. We might be able to sneak you into town and get you into a hotel room or something like that." The Kid smiled. "Maybe even get you that hot bath."

"I would be eternally grateful for that," she told him fervently.

Drake came along then, so they cut the conversation short. He had his arms full of dry cottonwood branches.

"While you two were gabbing, I got us some firewood," he said, but he didn't sound particularly resentful about having to take care of that chore.

They built a tiny fire, cooked biscuits and bacon, and heated up some leftover beans. The Kid knew he could wait until he rode into Gehenna and get a real meal, but that didn't seem fair, so he ate the same trail grub as his companions.

The sky turned a darker blue, then purple and black by stages. Stars winked into existence. The moon was still down but would rise later.

Drake let the fire burn down to embers before

he said, "I reckon it's late enough for you to start into town, Kid."

The Kid downed the last of the coffee in his cup. "I was thinking the same thing. Do you have any idea where I should start looking for Bledsoe? Any place he ever mentioned where he liked to spend time?"

"He talked about a cathouse called Rosarita's." With mocking courtesy, Drake added, "Begging your pardon for being crude, Miss Fletcher."

"Think nothing of it, Mr. Drake," Jillian said. "I was about to suggest that Mr. Morgan begin his search wherever there are whores and whiskey, since those are the things men care the most about."

The Kid chuckled. That steel was definitely showing through.

"Got any advice?" he asked Drake as he saddled one of the fresher horses.

"Yeah. Don't get yourself killed first thing. In other words, stay out of trouble that doesn't concern us."

"You think I'm liable to run into anything like that?"

"In Gehenna?" Drake grunted. "I'd say the odds are pretty good. Or pretty bad, depending on how you look at it."

The Kid finished tightening the cinches. "I'll steer clear of any ruckuses that break out. I'm just looking for Bledsoe, that's all."

Drake nodded. "That's right." He held out a hand. "Good luck, Kid."

The Kid wasn't fond of shaking hands with a

cold-blooded murderer . . . but his own hands weren't all that clean, he told himself. For better or worse, Drake was his partner for the time being. He gripped Drake's hand and shook.

When he turned to Jillian, she put her arms around him and hugged him before he could stop her. "Be careful, Kid," she urged. "Don't let anything happen to you."

He knew her words weren't motivated solely by concern for his safety. If he got himself killed, she would be alone, hundreds of miles from her home—such as it was—with a ruthless outlaw for her only company.

"Don't worry about me," he told her as he gave her an awkward pat on the back. "I may be back out here tonight. If I can't make it, I'll be back by tomorrow night at the latest."

As gently as possible, he disengaged himself from Jillian's arms and mounted up. Without looking back, he rode out of the little hollow and headed toward Gehenna, which was a scattering of yellow lights in the vast darkness along the border.

He began to hear music before he reached the settlement. Loud, raucous, and discordant, it was a blending of melodies from several different sources. He heard the tinny notes of a player piano from a saloon and the strumming of a guitar from a cantina. There was even a woman singing somewhere in a screechy, off-key voice.

As the music—if it could be called that—drifted to his ears, an assortment of aromas tickled his nose as a nocturnal breeze kicked up from the southwest. He smelled meat cooking, spiced with peppers and mesquite smoke, but an undercurrent of decay and horseshit lay beneath it. He could have sworn he smelled whiskey and unwashed human flesh, too, but that was probably just his imagination.

The Kid tugged the brim of his hat down lower over his face as he reached the eastern end of the street. He kept the horse moving at a slow, deliberate walk, as if he were just a drifting cowpoke, not going anyplace in particular and in no hurry to get there.

A stocky Mexican in a big straw sombrero sat on the driver's seat of a wagon parked in front of a general store while two more men loaded supplies into the back of it. The Kid veered his horse closer to the wagon and gave the driver a curt nod.

"Evening, amigo," he said, drawling the words out of the corner of his mouth. "You know where I can find a place called Rosarita's?"

"Sí, señor." The man pointed up the street. "In the next block, on the right."

The Kid nodded again. "Much obliged." He heeled the horse into motion.

Rosarita's was where the guitar music came from, he discovered as he rode up to the place. It was a two-story adobe structure, one of the largest buildings in town. A balcony with a wooden railing hung over the boardwalk in front.

The guitar player was an old man who sat in a ladderback chair tipped back against the front of the building. He strummed the strings with a skill that surprised The Kid. Knobby fingers danced nimbly, coaxing an elaborate melody out of the battered old instrument. The man nodded his head in time with the music and looked at nothing.

He couldn't look at anything, The Kid realized, because he was blind.

The hitch rails in front of the whorehouse were crowded. The Kid studied the rigs on the horses through narrowed eyes. Some of the saddles were American, the sort of functional rigs favored by working cowboys. Others were fancier, decorated with fringe and silver ornaments. Those would belong to the vaqueros from the other side of the border.

The Kid found an empty spot, swung down, and looped the horse's reins around the rail. He went up the two steps to the boardwalk and started past the old blind guitarist.

The man stopped playing and turned his head toward the sound of The Kid's footsteps. "Don't, señor," he said in a voice cracked and scraped raw by the years.

The Kid paused and was about to ask him why when a terrific slam of gun-thunder suddenly erupted inside Rosarita's.

Chapter 23

The Kid stepped back and his hand went to the butt of the holstered Colt on his hip. He was ready to hook and draw if any of the shots came his way.

The roaring volley lasted only a few seconds, then an echoing silence fell over the night. The shots had quieted everything else in Gehenna, too.

There was movement in the whorehouse. A man stepped up to the doorway and brushed aside the beaded curtain. He wore a flat-crowned black hat, a black vest, and leather wrist cuffs over a white shirt, and black whipcord trousers. His clean-shaven face looked like it had been whittled out of hardwood.

As he stepped out, he spotted The Kid standing on the porch and froze. "Looking for trouble, friend?" the man rasped.

The Kid shook his head and moved his hand away from his gun. "Not hardly." He hated to do anything that smacked of backing down, but he had come too far, risked too much, to get mixed up right away in a gunfight.

The man chuckled. "That's the smart answer." His eyes narrowed as he looked at The Kid. "Do I know you?"

"I don't think so. I just rode into town about a minute ago. Never been here before."

"Yeah, well, I've been lots of other places . . . but I reckon you just look a little like somebody I know." The man turned his head and added over his shoulder, "Let's go."

Three men followed him out of the whorehouse and down the steps to the horses lined up at the hitch rails. One was a lean, hatchet-faced man in range clothes, one was a dandy with the long, slim fingers of a gambler, and the last man out the door was huge and had long blond hair and a beard. He reminded The Kid of pictures he had seen in books about Vikings. That is, if Vikings had worn fringed buckskins.

All of them eyed The Kid coldly as they passed him. He knew he was looking at a band of killers.

The four men mounted up and galloped off. The Kid didn't see where they went, but the pounding hoofbeats stopped after only a moment, so he knew they hadn't left Gehenna. They had only gone to one of the other buildings.

Inside Rosarita's, a woman began to wail piteously.

"They are gone, no?" the old blind guitarist asked.

"They're gone," The Kid confirmed.

"You are fortunate that they already vented their

killing rage, amigo. If you had gone inside, you might be dead, too."

"Or some of them might be," The Kid said.

The old man's leathery face added some more wrinkles as he smiled. "Ho, ho! You have the fire in your belly, no?"

"I don't run away from a fight." The Kid paused. "You knew hell was about to break loose in there, didn't you?"

The old man didn't say anything, just inclined his head to show his agreement with what The Kid said.

"How did you know?"

"Because I cannot see, you mean? When the eyes go, the other senses strengthen to take their place. I heard the angry words and knew that Señor Cragg and his friends would have to spill blood."

"You were playing the guitar. How could you hear that?"

The old man's narrow shoulders rose and fell. "As I said, my other senses are stronger since the clouds came over my eyes."

"Cragg was the first one who came out?"

"Sí. Alonzo Cragg. You have heard of him?"

The name was vaguely familiar to The Kid. Cragg was a gunman and outlaw, rumored to be fast on the draw.

Evidently the rumors had some basis in fact.

"I've heard of him. What about the other three?"

"J.P. Malone, a man with a face like an ax. Clyde Woods, with the fancy clothes and the face of a man who seldom sees the sun. And the big one, the young giant, I know only as Dakota Pete."

"That's them, all right," The Kid said. "How do you know what they look like?"

"I have asked people to describe them to me. I know what many of the people in this town look like." The old man smiled again. "I know what the girls who work in Rosarita's look like, and I know the soft warmth of their breasts because from time to time they take pity on an old blind fool who can play the guitar."

The Kid grunted. "What's your name, old-timer?"

"They call me only Viejo. I had another name once, but it no longer matters."

Viejo . . . Old Man. It fit, all right, The Kid thought.

The wailing inside had increased, with several women joining in the cries of grief. Even though Viejo couldn't see him, The Kid nodded toward the door and asked, "What happened in there?"

"What happens all too often now. Men argued, and men died."

"The argument was over a woman?"

"What else? Although if it had not been that, it would have been something else. Men such as Cragg seek any excuse to spill blood. Death is like air and wine to them."

"Where did they go? It didn't sound like they went very far."

Viejo shook his head. "Not far. To Señor Harrison's saloon."

"Who's Harrison?"

"Cragg and the others work for him. They enforce his will on the town."

So this man Harrison had the settlement under his thumb. That was good to know, The Kid thought, but it didn't answer the question that had brought him there.

"What about a man called Bledsoe? Is he here in Gehenna?"

"A friend of yours, amigo?"

"I've never met him," The Kid said, "but I need to talk to him."

Viejo sighed. "Regretfully, I cannot help you. I know nothing of this hombre Bledsoe."

The Kid's spirits sank a little. The old-timer seemed to know everybody and everything about Gehenna. If he said Bledsoe wasn't there, it was a strong possibility the fugitive from Hell Gate had never made it that far.

Something could have happened to Bledsoe on the way, or he could have simply decided to go somewhere else, despite what he had told Carl Drake. Either way, it meant the long trip from New Mexico had been for nothing.

It was too soon to give up, The Kid told himself, regardless of what the old man said. According to Drake, Bledsoe had been a regular customer at Rosarita's. He ought to at least go inside and ask around.

The Kid took a step toward the doorway, then stopped again as Viejo said, "Señor, please . . ."

"What is it?" The Kid dug in a pocket for one of the coins they had found in the saddlebags of the dead outlaws. "I can give you something—"

"No, señor. I want for nothing. My songs and

my words I give freely. Only . . . a small boon, if you would."

"If I can," The Kid said.

"I would like to touch your face and let my fingers see you as only they can."

The Kid grimaced. He didn't like the idea of the old-timer pawing at his face. But he supposed it was a small enough favor to grant. "All right," he said.

Viejo set the guitar aside and stood up. He moved closer to The Kid. He was a head shorter, but he reached up and unerringly touched The Kid's cheek with his fingertips. His hand was dry and scaly, like the skin of a lizard, as he moved it across the younger man's features.

Viejo's eyes began to widen. *"Madre de Dios!"* he breathed. He passed his hand across The Kid's eyes, then suddenly jerked it back. *"El Diablo!"* he said. "You . . . you have the face of Satan himself!"

"That's the first time anybody's ever said that about me."

"You . . . you should leave this place. Nothing good can come of you being here."

"Sorry, old-timer. I won't be riding out until I'm good and ready. I've got business to take care of here in Gehenna."

"The Devil's business!"

"Maybe," The Kid said, as he stepped past the old man, who was making the sign of the cross with a trembling hand, and went into the whorehouse.

Chapter 24

Women were still carrying on in the parlor in which The Kid found himself. Three of them were on their knees next to the bullet-riddled corpses of three men, two Mexicans and one American. The Kid wondered if they were from one of those mule trains Drake had mentioned that carried ore from the mines in Mexico to the railroad in Tucson.

The mourning women were all Mexican, as were the others who stood around watching. They wore silk robes and not much else.

One of the wailing women climbed to her feet and threw herself at a man who stood by with a worried frown on his face. She began beating at his chest and cursing him in Spanish. She lapsed into English as she demanded, "Why did you not stop them? Why?"

The man was fat and middle-aged, with thinning brown hair and a brush of a mustache. He said, "How could I stop them? If I'd got in the middle of that, Harrison's butchers would've cut me down, too!"

The Kid pegged the man as the whorehouse's bouncer, whose job was to handle customers who got too drunk or started being too rough with the soiled doves. Interfering with professional gunmen like Cragg and the others would be beyond his capabilities.

The woman was too grief-stricken to accept that. She kept beating at the man's chest. He stood there and took it until a voice spoke sharply from a staircase leading to the second floor.

"That's enough, Julietta."

The woman stopped hitting the man. She stepped back, covered her face with her hands, and continued sobbing.

"Brady, have you sent for the undertaker?" the woman on the stairs asked.

The fat man nodded. "Yes, ma'am, I sure did. He ought to be here soon."

"Good. The ladies will be able to gain control of themselves easier once the bodies are out of here." She turned her head to look at The Kid. No one else in the room seemed to have noticed him as he stood just inside the doorway. "Who are you?"

She seemed to be in charge, which probably meant she was Rosarita. The Kid kept the surprise he felt off his face as he looked up at her. She didn't look like any Rosarita he would have expected. She was in her thirties, he guessed, and sleekly beautiful in a red gown that hugged her body.

She was also Chinese, or at least part Chinese, with smooth golden skin, almond-shaped eyes, and a mass of lustrous black hair piled high on her head.

The Kid lifted a finger to the brim of his hat. "I don't mean to intrude, ma'am. I figured to do a little business, but I got here just as the ruckus broke out."

He deliberately made himself sound like a cowboy. He didn't want to draw attention to himself by revealing his true background and education.

The woman regarded him solemnly and said, "You're lucky you didn't arrive a little earlier. You might have gotten in the way of a stray bullet."

"Yes, ma'am. I can't argue with that."

"Come back later," she said with a dismissive gesture. "We're closed for the time being." She nodded toward the dead men, as if their presence was reason enough for her decree.

"Actually, I'd like to talk to you for a few minutes, if that's all right. I could come upstairs—"

"I don't go with the customers," she snapped.

"But you *are* Rosarita?"

"That's the name I use now, yes. What business is that of yours?"

"I'm looking for someone you probably used to know."

She sighed. "You're going to be persistent, aren't you?"

Brady asked, "You want me to run this fella off, ma'am?"

"I doubt if you could," Rosarita said. "He doesn't look like he would run off easily." She lifted a hand to motion to The Kid. "All right. Come on. But I warn you"—her hand moved again and it held a small pistol that seemed to have materialized by magic—"if you're looking for trouble, you'll regret it."

The Kid shook his head. "No trouble, ma'am. You have my word on that." He moved past Brady and started up the stairs.

Rosarita kept the pistol in her hand as she turned and led the way to a bedroom furnished with a heavy four-poster bed and a low, leather sofa. It was more than the madam's bedroom. It was also her office, as evidenced by the big rolltop desk with several ledgers sitting open on it.

"Leave the door open," Rosarita said as she turned to face him again. "What do you want?"

As anxious as he was to find out about Bledsoe, The Kid satisfied another curious itch first. "How did you come to be called Rosarita?"

"You mean because I'm Chinese? I worked here, for the original Rosarita. Before she died, she told me she wanted me to take over the place and keep her name on it. I thought if this was going to continue to be Rosarita's, the woman who ran it should be known by that name, too." She slipped the gun back into the hidden pocket in her dress and turned to a sidebar. "Would you like something to drink?"

"No, thanks," The Kid said.

Rosarita picked up a decanter and poured a drink for herself into a squat crystal glass. She sipped it as she turned back to him.

"You didn't come here to ask me about my name. You wouldn't have been so insistent about that. Ask what you came to find out."

"I'm looking for work," he said. He had mentioned Bledsoe by name to the old man outside, which had been a mistake. He took a different tack with the woman.

The almond-shaped eyes narrowed as she studied him. "I don't hire men, except to keep things peaceful here in the house. You have the look of a man who would be a lot more capable of that than Brady . . . but I doubt if I could afford you."

"I'm not talking about working in a whorehouse. No offense."

She smiled coldly. "None taken. What *are* you talking about, then?"

"I reckon you know. Gun work. Gehenna's got a reputation as a wide-open town. I figured somebody around here might have need of my services. The madam of the best whorehouse in town generally knows all the men in town who have money."

She inclined her head in acknowledgment of that point.

"I was hoping you could point me in the right direction," The Kid went on.

She came closer to him. Now that he had a

better look at her, he saw she was older than he'd thought at first. Probably forty, although it was a well-preserved forty, especially for a woman who'd been in her line of work.

"The man you want to see," she said, "is Matthew Harrison. At least, that would be the case if he didn't already have several perfectly capable gunmen working for him."

"Cragg and the others I saw leaving the place, after they'd gunned down those three men in your parlor?"

"That's right. I'm afraid if you showed up at Harrison's and tried to take the place of any of them, you'd wind up as dead as those poor men downstairs."

"Maybe. But if Harrison's the only one hiring around here . . ."

Rosarita's lips twisted bitterly. "It's more than that. It's only been a few weeks since he showed up, but in that time, Harrison has taken over almost everything in Gehenna. Nobody knows what happened to George Hopkins, who owned The Birdcage Saloon before Harrison took it over and renamed it after himself. All the other businesses have to pay him a share of their profits now, or else bad things happen to them that no one can explain . . . but everyone knows who's behind them." She tossed back the rest of her drink. "Why the hell am I telling you all this? If you *did* wind up working for Harrison, you could tell him I was trying to stir up sentiment against him."

The Kid smiled wryly. "It sounds to me like he doesn't have any trouble doing that himself. I don't see how a man can take over a whole town with only four gun-wolves, though."

"Oh, he has a dozen other men working for him. Cragg, Woods, Malone, and Dakota Pete are just the worst of the bunch."

Something else she said had caught The Kid's interest. "You said Harrison's only been here in town for a short time?"

"A little over a month. That just goes to show you a lot can change in a hurry, if there are enough guns involved."

The Kid didn't doubt that. "Do you know where he came from?"

"No idea," Rosarita said.

"What does he look like?"

The madam tilted her head to the side and frowned as she gazed at The Kid. "That's it," she murmured. "There's something about you that seems familiar, and now I've finally figured out what it is. You look a little like him. Harrison, I mean. You're younger, and he has a beard, but there's a definite resemblance."

The Kid's heart slugged heavily in his chest. With an effort, he kept his face under control so it didn't reveal what he was feeling.

Bledsoe was in Gehenna. For some unknown reason, he was calling himself Matthew Harrison, but everything else fit. He had seized power in the border town and surrounded himself with

gunmen. Capturing him and taking him back
to Hell Gate wasn't going to be easy.

But The Kid had never expected it to be easy.
It was just one more challenge he would have
to meet.

He had the glimmering of an idea how he
might be able to do it.

The woman had moved closer to him, close
enough she was able to lift a hand and rest her
fingers lightly against his chest. She looked up at
him with dark brown eyes and said, "You should
stay away from Harrison's place. You don't need
to get yourself killed."

"A man's got to eat and have a place to stay."

"Stay here for a few days," she suggested.

"You've already got a bouncer."

She shook her head. "I didn't say I wanted to
hire you."

"I don't have enough money to afford to stay."

"You wouldn't have to pay." Her hand slid up
to his shoulder and stole behind his neck. He felt
the warmth of her breath on his cheek.

"You said you don't go with the customers."

"You wouldn't be a customer if you weren't
paying," she pointed out. She lifted her face to
his and pressed her mouth against his lips. When
she drew back a moment later, she whispered,
"Damn it, I've always had a weakness for a young,
handsome man . . ."

It was tempting. He couldn't deny that.
Rosarita was quite a bit older than him, but she
had a timeless beauty about her. It might be nice

to take some comfort with her. It wouldn't mean anything. Just some momentary pleasure to take the edge off what had been a rough few weeks.

"Sorry," The Kid said quietly as he took hold of her wrist and moved her hand from the back of his neck. "I appreciate the offer, but I'll have to pass."

Her face hardened. "The opportunity won't come around again, you know."

"I know. There may be some cold, lonely nights when I regret the decision and call myself a damned fool. But that's the way it is."

"You *are* a damned fool," she said. "You're going down there, aren't you? You're going to get yourself killed."

"No, I'm going to see a man about a job."

"You men and your guns," she said bitterly as she stepped back. "It always comes down to that, doesn't it?"

"Not always," The Kid said. "But often enough."

"Then go. Go on, damn you. If you live, don't come back here." She turned away. "I don't want to see you."

"Fine." He paused at the door. "I'm obliged for the information, and sorry about what happened downstairs."

"It was none of your doing. It'll happen again, as long as Harrison and his men are running things around here. And you . . . you'll either be one of them, or you'll be dead, soon enough."

There was a third option, The Kid thought, but

he couldn't explain that to her. Perhaps he could sometime in the future, if luck was with him.

He went downstairs. The soiled doves had all disappeared. Brady and the undertaker were carrying out the corpses and loading them into the back of a wagon.

The Kid stepped onto the boardwalk and turned in the direction Cragg and the other gunmen had gone earlier. His steps took him past the old man, who was sitting in the chair again and rubbing his fingers over the smooth wood of his guitar.

"El Diablo walks the night," Viejo said to The Kid's back. "The man who wears Satan's face."

The old man's voice trailed off into a muttered prayer.

Chapter 25

The saloon stretched the length of an entire block and had two entrances, one at the corner and one down the boardwalk in the middle of the block. A freshly painted sign hung from the awning and read: HARRISON'S SALOON—COLD BEER—GAMES OF CHANCE—DANCE HALL.

It was a full-service establishment, The Kid thought with a faint smile as he studied it from across the street.

Business was good. Men went in and out the batwinged entrance at the corner. The Kid looked through the big plate-glass front windows and saw a horseshoe-shaped bar in the center of the big room. To the right of the bar were tables where men sat and drank and flirted with the girls in short, spangled dresses who worked there. To the rear on the right was the open area where men could dance with the girls for a price. The player piano he had heard earlier was tucked into the corner. The tinny notes had stilled when the gunshots rang out down the street, but they were playing again.

To the left were poker tables, along with faro and keno layouts and a roulette wheel. Past the gambling tables was a staircase that led to the second floor. The girls probably earned some of their pay up there, too.

The room was brightly lit by oil-burning chandeliers decorated with cut glass. Overall, Harrison's was a little bigger and a little fancier than a lot of frontier saloons, but it was still a saloon. The Kid knew even without stepping in there what it would smell like—whiskey, stale beer, tobacco smoke, cheap perfume, and hair pomade.

To some men, that was the breath of life. Not to him. Being around that many people bothered him. He rode alone by choice, and for a good reason. He preferred the solitude of his grief.

Life just didn't seem to understand that. It kept dragging him into one mess after another. He would never be free of the current mess until he brought Bloody Ben Bledsoe—or Matthew Harrison as he was calling himself—to justice.

The Kid started across the street, pausing to let a group of vaqueros on their way to the saloon get there first and push through the batwings ahead of him. He followed them in, knowing their wide-brimmed, steeple-crowned sombreros would shield him from immediate view.

The Kid's eyes quickly surveyed the room from one end to the other, before anyone got a good look at him.

Alonzo Cragg and Dakota Pete stood at the bar, drinking. Clyde Woods, the gambler, was sitting at one of the poker tables, playing with several other men. The Kid didn't see J.P. Malone. And he didn't see anybody who looked the least bit like the face he saw, with or without a beard, looking out at him from the mirror when he shaved.

Bledsoe might be back in the office, or he might be upstairs.

One thing was certain: if he was at the saloon, a ruckus would draw him out.

The Kid ambled over to the bar. He could pick a fight with one of Bledsoe's top gun-wolves. If he survived, there was a chance Bledsoe might hire him to replace the dead man.

There was just as good a chance if he killed, say, Dakota Pete, the rest of Bledsoe's men would throw down on him. The Kid had plenty of confidence in his abilities, but he was realistic. He couldn't outshoot a dozen professional killers. He would get lead in several of them, no doubt about that, but they would down him, too.

There was no need to rush, he told himself. He was a long way from Hell Gate Prison, and none of the men who were after him knew where he was. He could afford to bide his time and wait for a better chance to work his way closer to Bledsoe.

Standing not far from Cragg and Dakota Pete, he nodded to the bartender and ordered a beer. The apron drew it, slid the foaming mug across the hardwood, and said, "That'll be four bits."

"For a beer?" The Kid asked with a surprised frown.

"For the coldest, best beer you'll find this side of Tucson, friend," the bartender said. "Anyway, that's the going rate, so take it or leave it."

The Kid pushed a couple of coins across the bar. "I'll take it." He picked up the beer and took a swallow of it. The bartender had overstated the case a little, but the beer wasn't bad.

From the corner of his eye, The Kid saw Dakota Pete nudge Cragg. The sullen gunman leaned back so he could look past his big companion. After a moment, Cragg picked up the bottle in front of him and splashed whiskey into a shot glass on the bar. He picked up the glass with his left hand and stepped away from the bar, turning toward The Kid.

"Hey," said Cragg, "aren't you the hombre we saw a little while ago when we were coming out of the China gal's whorehouse?"

The Kid set his mug on the bar, turned to look at Cragg, and nodded. "I think so."

"You follow us up here, mister? You looking for trouble?"

The Kid shook his head. "No. The madam said they were closed temporarily—something about having to haul out some corpses—so I figured it wouldn't do me any good to wait around there. I came up here looking for a drink instead."

Cragg nodded, seeming to accept the explanation. He held out the glass. "Have one on me."

"Thanks. I don't mind if I do."

The Kid reached for the glass.

Cragg dropped it as his other hand flashed toward the gun on his hip.

The Kid expected it. His eyes didn't follow the falling glass, as Cragg had figured they would. Instead, The Kid took a fast step forward and threw a hard left that smashed into Cragg's jaw just as the man's gun started to clear leather.

The powerful blow sent Cragg stumbling backwards into Dakota Pete, who instinctively grabbed him to keep him from falling. That occupied Pete's hands long enough for The Kid to palm out his Colt and level it at both of them.

"Don't try reaching for your guns," The Kid warned as he leaned against the bar. He thumbed back the hammer. "If the bartender or anybody else behind me gets the bright idea of walloping me over the head, my thumb's coming off this hammer. At this range, there's a good chance the slug will go clean through both of you."

Dakota Pete didn't go for his gun. Neither did anyone else. They weren't going to get mixed up in that when The Kid already had his gun cocked and aimed.

The punch had made Cragg groggy for a moment, but with a shake of his head to clear away the cobwebs, he straightened and snarled at Dakota Pete, "Let go of me, you big Scandihoovian lummox."

"Sorry, Lonzo," Pete rumbled. "I was just tryin' to keep you from fallin' down."

Cragg spread his feet a little, stiffened his

back, and tugged his vest back into place as he glared at The Kid. "What's the idea?" he demanded.

"You tried to draw on me," The Kid reminded him.

"I was just seeing what you're made of," Cragg snapped.

"Well, now you know."

"I wasn't going to shoot."

"Didn't have any way of knowing that," The Kid drawled.

"All right, all right." Cragg's gun had fallen to the sawdust-littered floor at his feet. "I'm going to pick up my iron now."

"Go ahead. Might be a good idea to do it careful-like, though."

Cragg bent and retrieved the revolver. He slid it into leather and then said, "You can lower that hammer now, cowboy. You're making me a mite nervous. Your thumb could slip."

"It never has yet," The Kid said. He carefully let the hammer down, lowering the gun until he held it at his side, but he didn't holster it.

"What's your name?"

He didn't see any reason not to tell the truth. "They call me Kid Morgan."

Dakota Pete said, "I think I've heard of him, Lonzo. He's supposed to be pretty fast."

"I'd say we saw that with our own eyes." To The Kid, he said, "I'm Alonzo Cragg. This is Dakota Pete."

The Kid gave them a curt nod and said, "I'd be

willing to bet you have quite a few friends in here, Cragg."

The gunman gave a minuscule shrug.

"If any of them decide to make a try for me, they might get me," The Kid went on, "but I'll get you first. If I'm going to hell, you'll be there to welcome me."

"Don't be so damn touchy," Cragg snapped. "I told you I wasn't going to shoot you. Nobody's going to bother you, Morgan." He raised his voice a little so everyone in the saloon could hear him as he said it. "Now, how about I buy you a drink? For real this time."

"All right," The Kid said. "You won't mind if I don't holster this shooting iron just yet?"

"Suit yourself." Cragg kicked aside the glass he had dropped and motioned for the bartender to bring a fresh one. He poured drinks for himself, Pete, and The Kid, who picked up his glass with his left hand.

"You sure are a distrustful cuss," Pete said.

"It's how I've lived this long," The Kid told him.

The three men drank. Around them, the atmosphere in the saloon slowly got back to normal after the tension that had gripped the room when it appeared guns might start to roar at any second.

"What brings you to Gehenna?" Cragg asked as he started to pour a second round.

"Same things that have taken me everywhere else I've been. A horse, and the need to earn some money."

"I hear some of the mines across the border in Mexico are hiring."

"I'm not a miner," The Kid said.

Cragg grunted. "No, I can see that."

"You know of anything else a man could do around here to earn some wages?" The Kid asked. Fate had presented him with an opportunity, and he wasn't going to let it pass him by.

Before Cragg could answer the question, The Kid heard a stirring in the crowd behind him. He had just started to turn when a man's voice asked, "Who's your new friend, Alonzo?"

The Kid continued the turn, moving smoothly and unhurriedly as if he didn't have a care in the world. He found himself looking straight into the face of the man he had come so far to find.

Bloody Ben Bledsoe.

Chapter 26

It wasn't exactly like looking into a mirror. There were some significant differences. Bledsoe's eyes were set slightly closer together. His nose was a little broader, his jaw slightly more angular, although it was hard to be sure about that because of the close-cropped sandy beard.

With the two of them standing together, no one except maybe blind Viejo would have any trouble telling them apart. If a person was only looking at one of them, however, it was understandable one might be mistaken for the other, The Kid thought.

"He says his name's Kid Morgan, boss," Cragg said.

Bledsoe nodded to The Kid. "I'm Matthew Harrison," he said. "This is my place." He gestured toward the glass in The Kid's hand. "Your first drink?"

"Tonight," The Kid confirmed.

"It's on the house, then." Bledsoe looked at

the bartender and the man nodded in understanding. Turning back to The Kid, Bledsoe
asked the same question Cragg had a moment or
two earlier. "What brings you to Gehenna, Mr.
Morgan?"

"We were just talking about that, boss," Cragg
said before The Kid could answer. "Morgan's
looking for work."

Bledsoe's eyebrows lifted a little. "Is that so?
What occupation do you follow?"

He was a well-spoken man, thought The Kid.
It was easy enough to believe Bledsoe had once
taught law at that university back east. How he
had gotten to Gehenna, Arizona Territory, from
William & Mary, was unknown, but that didn't
really matter.

"I don't have what you'd call an occupation,"
The Kid replied. "I pick up work here and
there."

Bledsoe nodded. "I see. And you're looking to
pick up work here in Gehenna?"

"If there's any to be had."

Bledsoe's voice hardened. "Well, you see, that
may be a slight problem. Men who do . . . your
sort of work . . . are employed by me, or not at all."

"You've got a monopoly on trouble?"

"You could say that," Bledsoe answered. "No
offense, Morgan, but how does a drifting gunman know about such things as monopolies?"

"I read a newspaper every now and then," The
Kid said with a shrug. He had almost slipped, revealing a knowledge of business that a man

whose main interests were whiskey, whores, and killing might not have.

"That's good. I believe people should be better-informed about this world we live in." Bledsoe made a curt gesture, and a second later the bartender handed him a glass that he'd filled from a bottle he took from underneath the hardwood. Brandy, The Kid guessed. Bledsoe drank from the glass, licked his lips appreciatively, and said, "So, do you want to work for me?"

"If you have something that needs doing, sure."

"That's the problem. I already have Alonzo and Pete here working for me, along with several other equally talented men. They've done such a good job bringing the town in line with my wishes there's really nothing left to do."

"In that case, I reckon I'll ride on in a day or two."

Bledsoe smiled. "Maybe something will come up between now and then. You never know."

The Kid shrugged again and lifted his glass. "Thanks for the drink."

"You're welcome." Bledsoe nodded. "See you around."

He moved away from the bar, walking through the big room, stopping here and there to speak to someone. The men he talked to looked nervous, as if they wanted to curry favor with him but were afraid of him at the same time. That was probably the case, The Kid thought.

Cragg said quietly, "If I was you, Morgan, I'd

give some thought to riding on out of town tonight, instead of hanging around for a few days."

The Kid arched an eyebrow. "Oh? Why is that?"

"Because like Mr. Harrison said, he's got plenty of help already. There's no reason for a man like you to hang around."

The Kid tossed back the rest of the whiskey and placed the empty glass on the bar.

"Having a little competition around worries you, does it, Cragg?"

The man's rawboned face flushed with anger. "Not hardly. Anyway, I wouldn't call it competition. You took me by surprise."

"Because I didn't fall for your little trick?"

Cragg didn't have an answer. He picked up the bottle from the bar and said, "Come on, Pete. I'm getting bored."

"Where are we goin', Lonzo?" the Viking gunman asked.

"I don't know, blast it! Somewhere else."

Pete's massive shoulders rose and fell. "Sure. Whatever you say."

Cragg and his companion went over to a table and sat down, leaving The Kid standing alone at the bar. The apron ambled up and nodded toward The Kid's empty glass.

"You want a refill on that, or another beer?"

The Kid shook his head. "No thanks. I think I'm done for the evening."

The bartender leaned closer and lowered his voice as he said, "I heard what Cragg told you. Don't worry about lookin' like he's got you buffaloed, mister. You'd be smart to get on outta town tonight, like he said. Men who don't pay attention to Cragg . . . well, they wind up dead, most times. Sometimes they weren't lookin' at what killed 'em, if you get my drift."

"So he's a backshooter?"

"I sure didn't say that. No, sir, I never did."

Despite the bartender's denial, the real message came through loud and clear. The Kid nodded his thanks for the warning and said, "I'm obliged for the advice, but my horse is tired and needs to rest. I'll be around."

"Suit yourself," the bartender replied in a bleak tone. He moved off, wiping circles on the hardwood with a damp rag.

The man had probably worked for the saloon's previous owner, George Hopkins, The Kid mused. The owner who had mysteriously gone missing just as "Matthew Harrison" had arrived in Gehenna and promptly taken over. The Kid had no doubt the man was either buried somewhere in the desert . . . or else he had been dumped so the buzzards picked his flesh and coyotes scattered the bare bones. The bartender and the others who had worked for Hopkins probably had no love lost for their current employer, but they were too afraid of Bledsoe and his gunmen to rock the boat.

The Kid finished the beer he'd been drinking earlier, then left the saloon. As he walked out, he was conscious of eyes following him and knew they belonged to Alonzo Cragg.

Cragg wouldn't let things rest. The Kid had humiliated him in front of everybody in the saloon. Enough people had seen it so the story would be all over town by morning—how the stranger who had ridden into Gehenna had laid out Cragg with one punch, beating him to the draw with his fist.

Despite Cragg's pose of friendliness following that incident, the thing would eat at him, nibbling away at his soul and his pride. The only way to stop the torment would be for The Kid to die. Out in public where everybody could see would be best, but Cragg would probably be willing to settle for an ambush, just as long as The Kid wound up dead.

The Kid turned toward Rosarita's place, where he had left his horse. He walked slowly along the street, giving Cragg plenty of time to come after him if that's what the gunman wanted.

It was a dangerous game he was playing. Cragg was fast. The Kid had seen that with his own eyes. He had been only a hair faster than Cragg. The next time, it might be Cragg who shaved off that whisker of a heartbeat first.

He sensed it was his chance to penetrate Bledsoe's inner circle. What he would do when and if he got there, he didn't know. But the more Bledsoe trusted him, the easier it would be to capture the man and take him back to face justice. It was a gamble worth taking.

The Kid wished he had eyes in the back of his head so he could see if Cragg left the saloon and followed him. He glanced back from time to time, trying not to be too obvious about it.

The third time he looked back, he saw a big figure lumbering after him. "Hey, Kid, wait up."

The Kid stopped and turned, frowning slightly. He hadn't expected Dakota Pete to come after him alone. Maybe Cragg had sent the big man to deliver an invitation to a showdown.

As The Kid came around, he saw that he had stopped in front of the pitch-dark mouth of a narrow alley between a hardware store and a saddle shop. For a split second he faced the alley mouth, and in that second a gun roared and flame lanced out of the gloom.

Instinct twisted him aside so the bullet whispered past him, close enough to tug at his sleeve. He whipped up his gun in the same heartbeat, and before the man in the shadows could fire again, two shots blasted from The Kid's revolver. The reports were so close together they almost sounded like a single shot.

The gun in the alley went off again, but the flame from the muzzle spouted downward at the ground. The Kid backed away swiftly, continuing to turn so he could cover both the alley mouth and Dakota Pete.

The Viking gunman had thrust his hands in the air and made no move toward the revolver on his hip. "Don't shoot," he said. "I ain't slappin' leather, Kid."

Alonzo Cragg stumbled out of the alley. The street was faintly lit but bright enough for The Kid to recognize the man's clothing. His body had jerked so violently as both of The Kid's slugs hammered into his chest, his hat had come off. He still had his gun in his hand and tried to lift it as he weaved forward a few stumbling steps. "You . . . son of a bitch," he rasped. "You've . . . killed me!"

"Drop the gun, Cragg," The Kid warned.

Cragg ignored him. The gunman summoned up the last of his strength to lift the Colt again.

The Kid shot him in the center of the forehead and the bullet slammed him backward. His gun flew from his hand and he landed with his arms and legs outflung in death.

Knowing that Cragg was no longer a threat, The Kid turned toward Dakota Pete again. The big man still had his hands up.

"I ought to kill you, too," The Kid said, "for helping him try to bushwhack me."

Pete shook his shaggy head. "I didn't know what Lonzo was plannin', Kid. You got to believe me. He just told me to wait a minute, then come after you and tell you he wanted to talk to you."

"And it was just a coincidence that you called out to me as I was passing this alley, so I'd turn around and he'd have a chance to shoot me from the front and make it look like he downed me in a gunfight."

"I don't know nothin' about that," Pete insisted.

The Kid didn't believe him, but it wasn't worth arguing about. He would be careful about turning his back on Dakota Pete in the future.

The street was starting to fill with people as the citizens of Gehenna came out to see what all the shooting was about. Quickly, The Kid replaced the three rounds he had fired in case he needed a full wheel again.

He spotted Bledsoe coming down the street toward him, followed closely by the other two gunhawks, Malone and Woods.

Now they would see how the hand played out, The Kid thought as he slid his gun back into leather.

Chapter 27

Bledsoe stopped a few yards away, glanced at Pete, and said disgustedly, "Put your hands down, for God's sake."

He turned his attention to Cragg, staring at the gunman's body for a second before he shook his head and looked at The Kid.

"It was a fair fight?" Bledsoe asked.

"Cragg got off the first shot," The Kid said, not mentioning how that shot had come from the concealment of a dark alley.

"That's true, boss," Pete put in.

"When I want to hear from you, I'll ask you a question," Bledsoe snapped. He went on to The Kid, "I was afraid of this when I heard about how you got the best of Cragg. He wasn't the sort of man to forget about something like that. Of course, if he had been, I probably wouldn't have wanted him to work for me."

"Probably not," The Kid agreed.

"The interesting thing is that with Cragg gone,

I need to hire somebody else. Are you interested in the job, Morgan?"

"Like I told you before, I'm always looking to pick up a little work."

Bledsoe motioned with his head. "Come on back to the saloon. We'll talk about it."

The Kid pointed down the street with his left hand. "I was on my way to get my horse."

"Go ahead. You can take it to the livery stable in the next block. There won't be any charge for taking care of the animal. The owner and I have an . . . arrangement."

The Kid nodded. "Sure."

"Then come to the saloon. There's an empty room upstairs you can use." Bledsoe glanced meaningfully at Cragg's body, which lay stark and bloody in the light from a lantern one of the townsmen had brought up.

Bledsoe went on, "Dakota, why don't you go with Mr. Morgan and make sure he finds the livery all right?"

"Sure, boss," Pete said with a nod.

The Kid didn't particularly want the company, but as long as the big Viking was with him, there was less chance of being ambushed by Bledsoe's other gunmen—if the offer of a job had been less sincere than it sounded.

"All right, everyone," Bledsoe said, raising his voice to address the crowd as if he were a lawman, "break it up and move on. The trouble's over."

In a way it was true that Bledsoe was the law there, just as Warden Jonas Fletcher had been the law at Hell Gate Prison. Gehenna was like everywhere else. The rule of law meant something only when it was backed up by force, or the threat of it.

The Kid started toward Rosarita's again, accompanied by Dakota Pete. As they walked along the street, Pete said, "I was tellin' the truth before, Kid. I didn't know Lonzo was gonna bushwhack you."

"He never pulled a stunt like that before?"

"Not with me helpin' him, he didn't," Pete insisted. "I don't know about anything Clyde or J.P. might've done. Them and Lonzo were pretty close. They rode together before, on other jobs."

"But not you?"

"Nope. Never met any of 'em before we all come to Gehenna."

The Kid indulged his curiosity. "How did all of you wind up here? What made you come?"

"Heard that a fella was puttin' together a bunch to come down here and take over," Pete answered bluntly. "I was up in Prescott, workin' on a deal there involvin' the railroad. It didn't turn out like it was supposed to, so I had to light a shuck outta there in a hurry. Things got a mite hot for me, if you know what I mean. When I made it to Tucson, I heard about Mr. Harrison's job and went to see him. He already had Lonzo and several others workin' for him. We hit it off, so I threw in with 'em."

Pete sounded like he was telling the truth, and The Kid was more inclined to believe him about not knowing exactly what Cragg had in mind, although he must have suspected something was up.

As they came to Rosarita's, Pete looked at the whorehouse and sighed. "I reckon we ain't wanted in there no more."

"The place is closed down right now, anyway," The Kid said. "What happened in there earlier?"

Pete waved a big hand. "Oh, it was just stupid. Those fellas were from one of those mule trains that come through here loaded down with ore. They'd picked out some girls, but Lonzo and J.P. decided they wanted the same girls and didn't want to wait for 'em. So Lonzo said they was goin' first, and those other fellas took exception to that, and before you know it, there was guns goin' off. Nothin' all that unusual."

The Kid nodded. The story was about what he'd expected.

"The China gal who runs the place'll be mad at us for gettin' blood on the rugs, I reckon," Pete went on. "The boss says we got to go along with what she says." He paused. "Don't tell him I said so, but I think the boss has got a sweet spot for that China gal. She pays him part of her profits like 'most everybody else in town, but I think he'd rather spark her than collect from her."

That was an interesting bit of information, The Kid thought as he filed it away in his brain. He didn't know if it would prove to be useful, but the more he knew about his enemies, the better.

He untied his horse and led it back up the

street. Pete pointed out the livery stable Bledsoe had mentioned. The proprietor, who emerged from his office and living quarters attached to the barn fuzzy-headed and bleary-eyed from sleep, woke up fast when he saw Dakota Pete. He also agreed to take good care of The Kid's horse without hesitation.

"He means it, too," Pete said as he and The Kid left the place and headed back toward the saloon. "My horse is in there, and the fella does a fine job of takin' care of it. The other boys' horses are there, too."

The Kid wasn't surprised that the liveryman went out of his way to care for the mounts belonging to Bledsoe's gunmen. To do otherwise would be to risk his life, or at least his livelihood.

Cragg's body was gone when they went past the spot where the gunman had died. The undertaker was having a busy night.

The Kid thought busy nights were probably pretty common in Gehenna since Bloody Ben Bledsoe had come to town.

Activity in the saloon had returned to normal. The player piano twanged away on some plaintive melody. The ball clicked around and around the roulette wheel, and men slapped cards down on the green felt of the poker tables. Men laughed and cursed, and saloon girls giggled.

Bledsoe was sitting at a large round table in the rear with Malone and Woods. He motioned for The Kid and Pete to come over and join them.

As The Kid approached, he kept a wary eye

on the two gunhawks. According to Pete, they'd been trail partners with Cragg in the past. They might be inclined to try to settle the score for him.

Bledsoe smiled. Malone and Woods didn't exactly follow his lead, but they didn't glare murderously at The Kid. Their faces were carefully neutral.

"Sit down," Bledsoe invited, waving The Kid into an empty chair. "Did you get your horse settled in over at the livery?"

The Kid nodded. "Yeah. Much obliged."

Bledsoe made a deprecating motion. "It's nothing. Always happy to help out one of my men."

"I haven't said I'd work for you," The Kid pointed out.

"No, but you need a job and I need a man with certain skills—skills which you've amply demonstrated tonight." Bledsoe reached for a bottle on the table. "Drink?"

The Kid shook his head. "I'd rather not let whiskey muddle my brain if we're going to be talking business."

"I'll take a drink, boss," Pete said. "It don't matter if my brain's a little muddled."

Woods muttered, "How would anyone ever know?"

Instead of taking offense at the thinly veiled insult, Pete chuckled and said, "Yeah."

Bledsoe shoved the bottle over to him. "Help yourself." To The Kid, he went on, "I've been talking to Clyde and J.P. here about you joining us, Morgan. They're not opposed to the idea."

"I'm glad to hear that," The Kid said dryly. "I was worrying about that very thing."

Malone's already thin lips tightened even more. He started to lean forward and opened his mouth to say something, but Bledsoe silenced him by moving a finger.

"I like for my men to get along," Bledsoe said. "We have enough enemies around here without fighting each other."

"You seem to be Gehenna's leading citizen. I wouldn't think you'd have any enemies."

"You know better than that, Morgan," Bledsoe chided. "No man is given power. He has to *seize* it. And you can't seize power without taking it away from someone else. That makes enemies."

The Kid nodded. "I suppose you're right."

Bledsoe clasped his hands together in front of him. "Right now, the people around here are like cattle at the start of a drive. It's not that hard to prod and poke them into going in the direction you want them to go. They don't want to suffer any. They don't even want to be inconvenienced. But just like a cattle drive, the longer things go on, the harder they're going to be to control. They're going to ask themselves why they're plodding along peacefully to the slaughterhouse. When that starts to happen, some of them will try to stampede." Bledsoe's voice hardened. "That's when we show them again who's really in charge, whatever it takes."

The Kid nodded. "You're right."

"Of course I'm right. What do you say, Morgan?

You want to sign on to help us keep things in line? The job pays a hundred dollars a month, but in the long run, there'll be an opportunity for all of us to make a lot more than that."

The Kid glanced at Malone and Woods and asked, "No hard feelings about what happened to Cragg?"

"Cragg made his own choice," Bledsoe said, "and my men only have hard feelings if and when I say they do. I'm willing to move on."

"In that case . . . I say the job's too good to pass up. You've got a deal, Mr. Harrison."

Bledsoe sat back in his chair, smiling. "Fine. You won't regret this, Morgan."

No, The Kid thought, *I won't regret it at all when you're hog-tied and on your way back to Hell Gate Prison to get what's coming to you.*

Chapter 28

Even after he had agreed to work for Bledsoe and settled the evening's business, The Kid didn't drink much, only one more beer. He pled weariness, which wasn't actually a lie, and said that if it was all right and his new boss didn't need him for anything, he was ready to turn in.

"Sure," Bledsoe replied with a nod. "You want one of the girls to go upstairs with you?"

"Maybe another time," The Kid said. "Tonight I'm just interested in sleep."

Bledsoe shrugged. "Whatever you want. Some men like to be with a woman after a killing."

"Not me," The Kid said.

"Well, any time you want one of them, just say the word. Men who work for me don't have to pay. The same is true down at Rosarita's."

"Like at the livery stable?"

"Something like that, yes," Bledsoe said with a smile. "The fact of the matter is, your money's not good for anything in this town from here on out, Morgan—which means your wages are profit, free and clear."

"That's a good arrangement."

"My men seem to think so." Bledsoe looked at Dakota Pete. "Take Morgan upstairs and show him the empty room at the end of the hall, Pete. He can bunk there."

"Sure, boss."

The Kid and Pete stood up.

"One more thing," Bledsoe went on. "Make sure somebody else knows where you are at all times. If there's trouble, any time of the night or day, I don't want to have to run around trying to find you. You're always on the job, understand?"

The Kid nodded. "Sure. For the next seven or eight hours, I'll be in that room upstairs."

"Good. Remember that."

As they started up the stairs, The Kid asked Pete, "This isn't Cragg's room I'm taking, is it?"

Pete shook his head. "Naw. Somebody'll have to clean Lonzo's gear outta his room. Probably J.P. They was closer friends than Lonzo and Clyde."

"I wouldn't want to take the room of a man I'd just killed."

"Well, that's just plumb thoughtful of you, Kid."

Pete took him to a small room at the end of the second-floor hallway. An iron bedstead with a bare straw-tick mattress on it filled up most of the floor space, leaving only enough room for a tiny table with an oil lamp on it and a single chair. A folded sheet and blanket were on the bed.

The Kid picked up the bedding and saw a

brown stain on the mattress. "What happened to the fellow who used to have this room?" he asked.

Pete rubbed his bearded jaw and looked uncomfortable. "Well, he, uh, got one of the gals who works here mad at him 'cause of somethin' he said or did. I don't know exactly what. She snuck in here one night whilst he was sleepin' and stuck him with a knife. That woke him up, of course, so he grabbed his gun and shot her 'fore he fell back in the bed and died. She made it back out into the hall and died there. Real shame. She was pretty."

"What about the man?"

"Oh, I didn't know him too well. It was just a few days after we'd all come to Gehenna. I reckon he was all right, but I ain't shed no tears over him."

The Kid nodded. It was the same sort of casually violent, tragic story that had been repeated over and over again on the frontier. A lot of people seemed to have little regard for life, their own or anyone else's.

After saying good night to Pete, The Kid put the sheet and blanket on the bed. It wouldn't be the first time he had slept in a place where blood had been spilled.

He propped the chair under the doorknob, then unbuckled his gunbelt and hung it over one of the bedposts so the butt of his revolver stuck up from the holster within easy reach.

After stripping down to the bottom half of a pair of long underwear, he blew out the lamp and stretched out on top of the bedding. It was a warm night, and the curtain over the open window barely stirred in a faint breeze.

After a few moments of lying there staring up at the darkened ceiling, The Kid sat up and swung his legs out of bed. He stood up, went to the window, and pushed the curtain aside so he could look out into the night.

There was no balcony outside the window, no easy way to reach it from the ground. He had forgotten to check earlier, and he chided himself for overlooking it. The logical part of his brain said that a man simply couldn't be vigilant every waking moment. It wasn't possible. But a man who lived by the gun had to be.

Like a wild animal, when he slept he had to den up in a place where no predators could get to him. In Gehenna, the predators were all two-legged, starting with Bloody Ben Bledsoe.

The window faced east. Somewhere out in the vast Arizona darkness he was looking at, Carl Drake and Jillian Fletcher waited for him. He hoped they were all right . . . and that Drake could be trusted with the beautiful young woman. He wished he could have gotten back to the camp.

Drake had been locked up in Hell Gate Prison, too. He might decide to get back at Jonas Fletcher by taking out his hatred on the warden's daughter. If that happened, sooner or later The Kid would kill Drake. Simple as that.

When the Kid rode into Gehenna he hadn't expected to be working a few hours later, for the very man he had come to find. Fate had taken a hand in the game very quickly, and The Kid knew he couldn't afford to pass up the chance that had been given him.

He would feel better about things, though, when he could see with his own eyes that Jillian was still all right. With a sigh, he let the curtain fall closed and went back to lie down on the bed.

It was quite a while before he went to sleep.

When The Kid went downstairs the next morning, he found Bledsoe and the man's inner circle of gun-wolves sitting at the same table where they'd been the night before, but they were eating breakfast instead of drinking.

Bledsoe waved him over. He said, "Join us, Morgan," and he motioned to the bartender, who evidently was serving as the waiter.

The man brought a cup of coffee to The Kid and told him that he'd have some food for him in a few minutes.

Bledsoe drank from his own coffee cup and asked The Kid, "Are you ready to get to work this morning?"

The Kid nodded. "Sure. What's the job?"

"The fellow who runs the blacksmith shop has gotten reluctant to pay the share of profits he owes me. He says he can't afford it. I'm going to send Dakota here to remind him that he can't afford *not* to pay up. I like to have two men handling these little jobs, just in case."

"I won't have no trouble with him, boss," Pete insisted.

"I know that," Bledsoe said, "but I still want to send Morgan with you."

Pete nodded reluctantly. "Sure. Whatever you say, Mr. Harrison."

"That's right. Whatever I say, goes."

The ham, eggs, and hashed brown potatoes the bartender brought to The Kid were surprisingly good. He commented, "You must have a real kitchen back there, and somebody who knows his way around it."

Bledsoe shook his head. "No, there's a café in the next block that supplies all our meals. You can stop in there any time you want."

"And eat for no charge?" The Kid asked with a wolfish grin.

"Exactly. You're getting the idea, Morgan."

The Kid had the idea, all right. Bledsoe, in his false identity as saloon owner Matthew Harrison, was really running Gehenna like a tin-plated little dictator. He ruled the settlement with an iron fist and hired guns.

Even if he hadn't needed to take Bledsoe back to New Mexico to clear his name, he would have enjoyed busting up the man's party and breaking Bledsoe's grip on the town.

After what had happened to Rebel, The Kid sometimes had his doubts about the whole concept of justice, but he knew what was going on there wasn't right.

While The Kid was eating, Clyde Woods toyed

with a deck of cards. From time to time he glanced at J.P. Malone.

The Kid saw those glances and knew he couldn't afford to trust the two men. They had been closer to Alonzo Cragg than anyone else in town, and he had a hunch sooner or later they would try to avenge their friend.

They would be careful about it, though. They wouldn't want to get on their employer's bad side. After all, Bledsoe had hired The Kid and promised him there were no hard feelings.

If they could work things out so some sort of fatal "accident" happened to him, The Kid didn't doubt for a second that Woods and Malone would do such a thing.

When they were all finished with breakfast, Bledsoe said to The Kid and Pete, "All right, the two of you can go see that blacksmith now. Don't come back until things are settled with him."

"You bet, boss," Pete said with a nod of his shaggy head. He pushed his chair back and stood up.

The Kid did likewise, knowing it was a test of sorts. He wanted to make good on it, wanted Bledsoe to trust him . . . making it much easier when the time came to make his move.

He could feel Woods and Malone still watching him as he and Pete left the saloon. If the opportunity presented itself, they just might make an attempt against him right away.

"The blacksmith shop's down yonder," Pete said, pointing to the western end of town. "The fella's name is Bonham. He's pretty big."

Blacksmiths usually were, thought The Kid. It was a job that required a lot of strength.

"Not as big as me, though," Pete added with a touch of pride in his voice.

As they approached the squat, open-fronted blacksmith shop, The Kid heard a hammer ringing against an anvil. It was a familiar sound, comforting in a way because it smacked of normalcy, something that was probably in short supply those days in Gehenna.

The sound stopped short, as they came up to the building. A red glow came from the open door of the forge and heat washed from it.

The man who stood behind the anvil holding a short-handled sledgehammer wasn't wearing a shirt, although a thick leather apron covered his bare chest. Thick black hair curled out from under the apron. His head was covered with a thatch of the same sort of hair, and a beard jutted from his jaw. He was a little shorter than Dakota Pete, but his shoulders were just as broad and bulged with muscle in the same way.

Light and dark, The Kid thought. Pete and the blacksmith were almost like opposite sides of the same coin.

"Hey, Bonham," Pete began, "Mr. Harrison sent us to have a talk with you—"

The blacksmith interrupted with a rumbling roar of anger. He lunged around the anvil, raised the hammer, and rushed toward Pete with the tool held high, poised to descend with bone-crushing force.

Chapter 29

The Kid's first instinct was to draw his gun and put a slug through the blacksmith's leg, knocking Bonham down before he could smash Pete's skull with the hammer. But Bonham was just an honest working man defending what was his own, The Kid reminded himself.

Pete reacted quickly to the danger. He twisted to the side with surprising agility for such a big man, ducking out of the way as the hammer came down. The blow missed him and left Bonham off balance.

The next second, Pete tackled the blacksmith, driving him backward and lifting him off his feet in an amazing display of strength. It was like two of the legendary Titans of old engaging in mythological combat. Both men crashed to the ground in front of the anvil.

The Kid was a little surprised that the earth didn't shake under his feet from the impact of the massive bodies.

Bonham swung the hammer at Pete again, but Pete jerked his left hand up and grabbed the blacksmith's wrist in time to keep the blow from landing. The long, corded muscles in his arm bunched like steel cables under the buckskin shirt as he strained to keep Bonham from braining him.

At the same time, Pete's right hand darted at Bonham's throat and closed around it. The fingers dug into the flesh under the thick black beard.

Bonham's eyes widened grotesquely. He pounded at Pete's head with his free hand, but Pete just drew his neck down and hunched his shoulders so he was able to shrug off the blows.

A man riding by on the street reined his horse to a stop and stared at the ruckus for a moment, then abruptly kicked his mount into a run and took off, shouting, "Fight! Fight! Fight at the blacksmith shop!"

Even with the town in a grip of an outlaw tyrant, people still reacted to a fight going on, The Kid thought. He moved around, circling so he could get a better view of what was going on.

Bonham changed his tactics and used his free hand to gouge at Pete's eyes. Pete twisted his head away from the clawing fingers, causing his grip on Bonham's wrist to slip.

The hammer thudded against Pete's shoulder. The blow didn't have much force behind it, but the hammer weighed enough to make it hurt. Pete howled in pain.

Bonham heaved up from the ground, arching

his back as he toppled Pete off him. The two men rolled over and over as they wrestled and punched at each other. A small cloud of dust rose around them.

The Kid spotted the hammer lying on the ground and realized Bonham must have dropped it. He darted forward and grabbed the hammer, intending to sling it out of reach so that the blacksmith couldn't get his hands on it again.

The Kid grunted with effort as he lifted the hammer. It weighed more than he'd thought. He had to grab hold of the handle with both hands and pivot with his body to sling it into the back of the shop, past the forge.

Bonham had wielded the hammer almost like it was a toy.

As The Kid turned back toward the combatants, he saw they had struggled to their knees. They continued to slug away at each other, absorbing terrific punishment even as they dealt it out.

The Kid thought about slipping his gun from its holster, coming up behind Bonham, and walloping the blacksmith. But it seemed like a cowardly thing to do, and something inside him rebelled against it.

Maybe Pete would win the fight, he told himself as he continued to watch.

He wasn't the only spectator. A crowd was gathering in the street in front of the blacksmith shop. Some of the men yelled encouragement to Bonham as they danced around excitedly.

Even though Pete was slightly bigger than Bonham, his punches lacked the piledriver force of the blacksmith's blows. The Kid saw Pete's arms begin to sag slightly. He was moving slower, too. The epic battle was taking its toll on him.

Finally, Pete failed to block one of Bonham's huge, knobby fists. It crashed into his jaw and sent him sprawling on his back, stunned.

Bonham heaved himself upright and started to swing around slowly toward The Kid.

The Kid had considered lacing his fingers together and using both hands as a club to land a devastating blow on Bonham. Unfortunately, hitting the blacksmith in the jaw would be like punching that anvil, and even if he succeeded in knocking Bonham down, he would probably break every knuckle in his hands in the process.

And knocking Bonham down was not the same as knocking him out . . . so, against his best instincts, as Bonham turned, The Kid drew his gun, stepped up, and slammed the Colt into the side of the blacksmith's head as hard as he could.

Bonham's eyes rolled up in their sockets. His knees folded, dropping him to the ground. As Bonham swayed for a second, The Kid stepped out of the way. Bonham toppled forward, landed facedown in the dirt, and didn't move.

The Kid glanced toward the street and saw the hostile looks on the faces of the crowd. He didn't care. He wasn't in Gehenna to win friends. He wanted to take Bledsoe back to Hell Gate and clear his name. Any good he did the citizens of Gehenna was just coincidental, he told himself. "Break it up," he snapped, sounding like Bledsoe had the night before. "Go on about your business."

The townspeople did so, reluctantly walking away from the blacksmith shop, but not without glaring some more at The Kid first.

He went to where Dakota Pete had fallen and knelt at the side of the big Viking gunman.

Pete's eyelids were fluttering. He moved his arms and legs around a little as awareness came back to him.

The Kid put a hand on his shoulder. "Pete," he said. "Pete, can you hear me?"

Pete rolled onto his side and groaned. "Oh, Lord!" he said. "What . . . what the hell happened?"

"Bonham knocked you out for a minute, that's what happened," The Kid told him with a faint smile on his face.

"Aw, hell!" Pete struggled into a sitting position. "I can't believe I let that big bastard whip me."

"Don't worry. It was a pretty even fight most of the way."

Pete leaned to the side and looked past The Kid at the blacksmith's senseless form stretched on the ground. "What happened to him? Who knocked him out?" Pete lifted his eyes to The Kid. "Surely it wasn't—"

"Me?" The Kid said. "Well, yeah, it was." He hefted the heavy Colt revolver. "But I had a little help."

"Oh." Pete nodded in understanding. "I get it now. You pistol-whipped him."

"Yeah, and I'm not proud of it. But I thought that would be better than breaking every bone in my hands and probably getting my head handed to me, as well."

Still holding the gun, The Kid straightened and turned toward Bonham. The blacksmith had begun to stir. It was amazing that anybody could have taken as much punishment as he had and not be unconscious for hours.

"If you can get up, help me turn him over," The Kid said to Pete, assuming command without even thinking about it. In his life as a wealthy businessman, he had been used to giving the orders, and that tendency still cropped up from time to time.

Pete climbed heavily to his feet. He was still a little unsteady but was able to reach down and take hold of Bonham's shoulder. With a grunt of effort, he rolled the massive blacksmith onto his back.

The Kid knelt and put the barrel of his gun under Bonham's beard, bearing down enough to dig the muzzle into the man's throat.

After a moment, Bonham forced his eyes open and gasped. He seemed to understand what the cold ring of metal prodding his neck was.

"That's right," The Kid said. "All I have to do to blow a chunk of your head off is pull the trigger. So you'd better not move, Bonham."

"Wha . . . what do you want?" rasped the blacksmith.

"You know why we're here, otherwise you

wouldn't have jumped us." The Kid's voice was cold as ice. "You've been giving trouble about living up to your responsibilities."

"I don't have any . . . responsibilities . . . to that snake Harrison!"

"That's where you're wrong. Things are different now in Gehenna. If you want to do business here, there's a price. You can pay it, or get out."

"Or die," Pete added ominously.

"Bonham here is too smart for that," The Kid went on. "He knows that part of something is better than all of nothing. And a dead man can't make *any* money. So why don't you show up down at the saloon with what you owe by, say, sundown tomorrow? That gives you a little time."

"Go to . . . hell," Bonham ground out.

The Kid pressed harder with the gun barrel. "You think it over," he advised softly. "You just think about it."

Then he pulled the Colt away and stood up with the lithe motion of a snake uncoiling. "Come on, Pete. I think he got the message."

The Kid and Dakota Pete backed away from the blacksmith.

Bonham sat up and glowered at them as he lifted a big hand to massage his sore neck. Bruises were already starting to form on his face where Pete's fists had battered him.

The same sort of bruises were beginning to be visible on Pete's face.

The Kid didn't holster his gun until he and his companion had turned toward the saloon. As they walked along the street, he was aware of people staring at them.

He thought about the old saying and was glad that looks couldn't kill. If they could, he and Pete would be buzzard bait.

"I can't believe he beat me," Pete muttered. "Nobody beats me."

"It happens to the best of us," The Kid said. "Cragg was fast, but I was faster. There are men out there faster on the draw than I am."

"That's a little hard to believe."

"Believe it," The Kid said, thinking of his father, Frank Morgan, the notorious Drifter. "There's always somebody faster, bigger, stronger. That's just the way life is."

"Maybe so, but I don't have to like it." Pete shook his head. "I sure hope the boss don't hear about what happened."

"He probably will. A lot of people saw the fight. Word will get back to him."

"Then you'll look good, and I'll just be a loser."

"Don't worry," The Kid told him. "If Harrison asks me about it, I'll tell him I never would have been able to handle Bonham if you hadn't taken him down a notch first."

"You'd do that, Kid?"

"Sure."

"That's mighty nice of you." Pete hesitated, then went on, "I got a hunch that when the boss hears about this, he's gonna make you his segundo, just like Lonzo was. That's liable to make J.P. and Clyde even more mad at you for killin' him."

The Kid nodded. "I'd already thought about that. I'm going to need eyes in the back of my head as long as I'm around here."

A big hand slapped into the middle of his back, knocking him forward a step. "Don't worry, Kid," Pete said with a big grin. "You got me for that."

Chapter 30

As The Kid had predicted, Bledsoe had already heard about the fight at the blacksmith shop by the time he and Pete got back to the saloon.

"That's why I wanted two people to handle that chore," Bledsoe said as he stood at the bar and talked to The Kid and Pete. Malone and Woods weren't around, as far as The Kid could tell.

"He got in some lucky punches, boss," Pete said.

Bledsoe lifted an eyebrow. "Quite a few lucky punches, from what I heard," he commented. "But don't worry about it, Dakota. From the sound of it, you and Morgan here make a good team. Why don't you stick together?"

Pete beamed. "That sounds mighty good to me."

"Sure," The Kid said as he nodded. He wasn't too happy about the partnership, despite the smile he put on his face. Bledsoe's insistence on always knowing where his men were was already making it difficult for The Kid to get out of town and rendezvous with Drake and Jillian. He needed to talk to them if they were going to figure out how to grab Bledsoe and get him out of Gehenna and back to Hell Gate.

There was nothing he could do about it at the moment, although an idea had begun to play around in the back of his head. "Anything else we can do for you now, boss?" The Kid went on.

Bledsoe shook his head. "No. I'll let you know if I need you for anything. Until then, just hang around here at the saloon or down at the café."

The Kid nodded in understanding.

Pete was pretty good company, friendly and easygoing and full of stories about growing up in North Dakota with his Norwegian grandparents. His parents had both been killed by Indians when Pete was just a boy.

The Kid pretended to be paying attention as he sat at one of the tables with the big Viking, dealing hands of solitaire with a deck of cards that someone had left lying on the green felt.

In reality, he was working on the plan he'd hatched to get out of Gehenna without Bledsoe knowing about it.

At midday, he and Pete walked down to the café, which was run by a middle-aged couple who gave them frightened, resentful glances from time to time while they were eating.

The Kid wanted to pay for the meals when he and Pete left, but he knew that the sort of man he was pretending to be wouldn't do that. A callous, mercenary gunman would be only too happy to take advantage of the chance for free meals.

Later on, if there was a chance, he would see to it that the couple got paid something for all the food they'd had to dish out to Bledsoe's hired killers. The Kid vowed to make things right with Bonham, the blacksmith, too.

As they strolled back toward the saloon, The Kid asked, "Have you ever paid a visit to Rosarita's, Pete?"

Pete grinned. "You mean the whorehouse run by that Chinese gal with the Mex name? You know I been there, Kid. You saw me there last night."

"Yeah, that's right," The Kid said, pretending that he'd forgotten about that . . . and the dead men on the floor of Rosarita's parlor. "What about the girls? Are they any good?"

"Sure. They're soiled doves, 'bout like what you'd find anywhere else, I reckon."

"I was thinking I might go down there this evening."

"Mr. Harrison said you and me was supposed to stay together."

The Kid chuckled. "Well, hell, Pete, you could come along, too, couldn't you?"

Pete thought it over. His grin slowly widened.

"I don't see why not," he said.

"Not in the same room, though," The Kid warned. "A man needs privacy for some things."

"Oh, yeah, sure. Both of us bein' there in the whorehouse at the same time, that's close enough to stayin' together."

"That's what I thought," The Kid said with a

nod, glad that Pete was falling in line with his plan without giving him any trouble.

All he had to do was convince Rosarita to cooperate.

The day was a long one, its monotony broken only by the appearance of Bonham at the saloon late that afternoon. The blacksmith had taken off his apron and put on a shirt, but otherwise he looked the same. He turned his bruised face from side to side, scowling as his gaze touched The Kid and Pete where they sat at one of the tables.

Then Bonham marched up to the bar and plopped down a canvas poke on the hardwood. The Kid heard coins jingle, even from across the room.

"Where's Harrison?" Bonham demanded of the bartender.

"*Mister* Harrison is back in the office. You want me to fetch him, Theo?"

"I damn sure do," Bonham rumbled.

"Hang on."

The bartender went through the door at the end of the bar and came back a moment later with Bledsoe. Bonham gave the poke a shove that sent it sliding down the bar toward him. It came to a stop in front of Bledsoe.

"There's your blood money, Harrison," Bonham said.

The Kid stayed in his chair, apparently casual.

He saw the anger smoldering in Bledsoe's eyes. The man hadn't gotten the nickname Bloody Ben for no reason. He put up a smooth façade, but underneath it he was just another outlaw.

"You should show some respect, Bonham," Bledsoe said. "I'm just trying to make this town a better place."

"Better for you, you mean," the blacksmith snapped. "Anyway, there's the money." He turned away from the bar to start out of the saloon.

Bledsoe stopped him by saying, "I'll expect the same amount next week, plus twenty more dollars."

Bonham stared at him for a second, then exploded, "Hell, I don't think I made twenty dollars over and above what's in that poke all week!"

"That's not my problem," Bledsoe said. "I guess you'll just have to work harder."

"There ain't that many horses and mules in these parts that need be shod."

"Again, you'll have to worry about that, not me."

Bonham looked like he wanted to bound across the floor, grab Bledsoe by the neck, and squeeze the life out of him. The Kid was ready to stand up and stop Bonham from doing that if the blacksmith tried it, and so was Pete. In fact, he looked eager for an excuse to have another scrap with the blacksmith.

But then Bonham's broad shoulders sagged in defeat. "All right, all right," he muttered as he turned toward the batwings again. "You'll get your money."

"I thought so," Bledsoe said with a smirk directed at Bonham's back.

When the man was gone, Bledsoe came over to the table and sat down at one of the empty chairs.

"These people just don't understand," he said as he slipped a cigar from his vest pocket. "They're like sheep or cattle. They were put here to benefit their superiors." Bledsoe put the cigar his mouth, clamped his teeth on it, and continued around the cylinder of tobacco, "You understand, don't you, Morgan? You strike me as a man who's had some education."

The Kid shrugged. "I just go along to try to get along, boss," he said.

Bledsoe jerked a thumb at the bar and said, "Go get us some beers, Dakota. Take your time about it."

"Sure, boss," Pete said as he lumbered to his feet.

The Kid kept his face carefully expressionless. It appeared Bledsoe wanted to talk to him in private for some reason.

When Pete had gone over to the bar, Bledsoe said quietly, "I sense a kindred spirit in you, Morgan. You might not know it to look at me now, but *I'm* an educated man. In fact, I once taught law at a famous university back east."

"I don't doubt it," The Kid said.

"You don't, eh?" Bledsoe leaned forward. "Well, what would you say if I told you that I grew up in these parts? I spent a lot of time in this jerk-water town when I was a young man. What's really sweet about that is none of these bastards even remember me!"

The Kid wasn't sure why Bledsoe had decided to tell him all of that, but he wasn't going to stop the outlaw.

"Of course, I had a different name then, and I didn't have the beard," Bledsoe went on. "Nobody gave a damn about me. I was just some starving kid. But I left and made something of myself, no matter what they thought of me."

"Sometimes when a fellow has it too easy, it's not good for him," The Kid said.

Bledsoe jabbed the cigar at him. "Exactly! I knew what it was like to be poor, and that helped me to get rich."

"Teaching at some university?"

"No, the getting rich came later," Bledsoe replied with a shake of his head. "I thought I'd be satisfied just making a life for myself where people respected me." A hint of bitterness edged into his voice. "I found out that people don't really respect a man because of how smart he is or how much education he has. There are only two things people respect, Kid, and they're actually variations of the same thing: money and power."

"What about a gun?"

Bledsoe shook his head again. "It's not the gun they respect. It's the power of life and death behind it."

"You may be right, boss."

"I know I'm right," Bledsoe said as he leaned

back in his chair and chewed on the unlit cigar again. "I proved it by coming back here and using a different name as I seized power. I'll let you in on my plan, Morgan. I'm going to bleed this town dry. This town, and everybody in it. And then, when there's nothing else I can take from them, I'll tell them that it wasn't Matthew Harrison who ruined them. No, sir. It was Ben Bledsoe. Ben Bledsoe, the son of that old rumpot Silas Bledsoe, the town drunk. The town joke. If I'd stayed here, I would have inherited that position from him. That's why I had to get out."

For a moment, The Kid didn't say anything. Then, "That's quite a story, boss. I'm thinking you don't want me telling anybody about it."

"That's right." Bledsoe's lips drew back from his teeth in a grimace. "If you tell anybody, I'll kill you myself, Morgan. I'll make sure you take a long, hard time dying, too."

The Kid shook his head. "You don't have a thing to worry about. This is a good setup. I don't want to ruin it."

"You'll keep your mouth shut, then. I'm not sure why I told you all that, anyway. I just get . . . tired . . . of being surrounded by people who have never been anywhere and never done anything worth mentioning. Like I said, you strike me as a man with some education. But if you don't want to talk about it, that's all right."

"Maybe someday," The Kid said.

"Sure. Whatever you want."

Pete came back over with the beers then, the tray with the mugs on it dwarfed by his big hands.

"Looked like you fellas was havin' quite a talk," he said. "What'd I miss?"

"Nothing much," The Kid said. "I was just telling the boss that you and I plan to go down to Rosarita's tonight."

"Yeah," Pete said as a look of anticipation lit up his eyes. "Is that all right with you, boss?"

Bledsoe took the cigar out of his mouth and waved the hand that held it in an expansive gesture. "Of course. Have a good time. I'll know where to find you if I need you."

The Kid hoped that situation didn't arise, because what Bledsoe had just said wasn't strictly true.

He was going to Rosarita's with Pete . . . but he wasn't going to stay there.

Chapter 31

After supper at the café, The Kid and Pete headed down the street toward Rosarita's. The sun had set almost an hour earlier, and stars had come out in the sable panoply of the sky overhead.

Something was nagging at The Kid's brain. "Do you know where Malone and Woods are?" he asked Pete. He hadn't seen the two gunmen around since early that morning.

"Nope," Pete replied with a shake of his head. "Could be they're off doin' somethin' for the boss. Or they could just be holed up somewhere drinkin'. J.P.'s got a real fondness for that Who-hit-John. He goes on a bender now and then."

The Kid nodded. Pete's explanation was certainly reasonable, but he would have felt better, knowing exactly where Malone and Woods were.

The blind guitar player Viejo wasn't on the porch, but Rosarita's was open for business again. When the two men went into the parlor, The Kid saw that the blood had been scrubbed up off the floor. He could still see the ragged crimson stains in his mind's eye, along with the bullet-riddled bodies from which the blood had leaked. Quietly, he asked Pete, "Did you do any of that shooting in here last night?"

"Naw. I can handle the gun work when I have to, but I ain't all that fond of it. That was the other fellas' doin'."

The Kid nodded, for some reason glad to know that Pete hadn't participated in the massacre. The big Viking was an outlaw and a hired killer, but The Kid felt a certain degree of liking for him, anyway. He didn't seem quite as cold-blooded as the others.

Several young Mexican women lounged around the parlor in various stages of undress. They smiled in welcome at the two men. A couple got up from a brocaded divan and came over to greet The Kid and Pete.

"You wish to be entertained this evening, señores?" one of them asked. She was short and stocky, with a definite earthy beauty about her. Her companion was taller and more slender. They looked like they might be sisters.

"That's right, little darlin'," Pete replied with a big grin. "You reckon you're up for the chore?"

"You're the one who will have to be up for it, muchacho," the woman said as she leaned closer to Dakota Pete, who was practically licking his lips in appreciation of the cleavage displayed in the soiled dove's silk shift.

"Oh, I am," he declared. "You damn well betcha I am!"

The Kid said, "Before we go upstairs, I need to talk to Rosarita for a minute."

The taller of the two whores shook her head and said, "She don' go with the customers, señor. But I'll be plenty of woman for you, you'll see."

"I still want to talk to her."

The woman sighed and called, "Brady!"

The fat bouncer came out of another room. He frowned at The Kid and asked, "Don't I know you?"

"I was here for a little while last night. I went upstairs and talked with Rosarita."

"Oh, yeah," Brady said. "I remember now. You come back to sample our girls?"

"Yeah, in a minute, as soon as I talk to Rosarita."

Pete asked, "How come, Kid? Is there a problem?"

"No, no problem," The Kid replied smoothly. "We just hit it off last night, and I want to say hello to her."

"That can wait," Pete said. He was starting to look impatient.

The Kid pasted a smile on his face. "No, I'll be too worn out afterward." He slid an arm around the waist of the taller whore. "I think this pretty little señorita is going to take all of my strength to handle."

She giggled and turned so that the soft, warm

mound of her breast pressed against his arm. "You are right about that, señor," she said.

"Yeah, fine," Brady said. "Come on upstairs."

"What about me and this gal?" Pete asked as he draped an arm over the shoulder of the shorter whore and fondled one of her breasts through the shift. "Reckon we can go ahead and get started?"

"Sure, have a good time," The Kid said. "Don't expect to see me for a while, though." He squeezed the woman with him. "I've got lots of ideas I want to try out, so I reckon I'll be up there for a while. You can just wait for me down here if you get through first, Pete." He leered at the other soiled doves in the room. "I reckon the company will be pretty good."

"You're damn right," Pete said. He tugged the shorter woman toward the stairs. "Come on, honey."

As they all started up to the second floor, the woman with The Kid leaned her head on his shoulder. "There are some things I don' do, mister," she said. She giggled again. "There must be. But I ain't foun' 'em yet!"

While Pete and his companion for the evening went off into one of the rooms, Brady knocked on the door of Rosarita's bedchamber and office.

"Fella out here wants to see you, ma'am," he called through the door.

The door opened a moment later. Rosarita looked out with a frown on her attractive face.

"Who—" Her almond-shaped eyes fell on The Kid. "You again," she said.

"I just need a minute of your time," he told her.

Rosarita looked like she was going to tell him to go away and not bother her, but then she shrugged and relented. "All right." She stepped back a little. "Come in."

The taller whore squeezed The Kid's arm, pointed to another door, and said, "I'll be right in there, honey, waiting for you. And I'll be *ready*."

He gave her a playful little swat on the butt as she started down the hall.

The smile dropped off The Kid's face as he stepped into Rosarita's room and she closed the door behind him.

"What do you want?" she asked sharply.

"A favor."

"I offered you a favor last night. You weren't interested."

"Not that kind of favor," The Kid said. "I want you and the gal I brought up here to do something for me."

Rosarita's eyes widened. She said something in Chinese that was probably a curse. She looked like she was about to yell for Brady when The Kid held up a hand to stop her.

"Whatever you're thinking, that's not it," he told her. "I want the two of you to pretend that I'm here for the next couple of hours."

"What do you mean, pretend you're here? You *are* here."

"Yeah, but I won't be, if you've got some back stairs and a way out of here where nobody will see me leaving."

Understanding began to dawn in Rosarita's eyes. "I heard that you killed Alonzo Cragg and then took his place working for Matthew Harrison."

"That's sort of the way it worked out, all right," The Kid admitted.

"I also know that Harrison likes to keep pretty close tabs on his men. You told him you were coming here tonight, but you really want to go somewhere else."

"Right again."

"Are you double-crossing Harrison?"

"That's something I'd rather not discuss," The Kid said. Let her draw her own conclusions, he thought.

Rosarita did. She drew in a breath and said, "I could sell you out to him, you know."

"Maybe you could. He might not believe you."

"If you weren't here, where you said you'd be, that would be proof, wouldn't it?"

"I suppose. But you don't have any reason to do that."

"Why not?" she asked. "Harrison might pay me for the information, or make me pay less. Either way, it's more money for me."

"Right now it is," The Kid said. "Over the long run, Harrison's going to suck all the life out of this town like a leech."

Rosarita looked at him intently for a long moment before nodding. "You're probably right about that," she said. "Just what is it you're planning?"

"It's better if you don't know that."

"Better for who? Me or you?"

"Everybody," The Kid said. "Everybody except Harrison and his men."

Again she regarded him for a moment. "You're putting a great deal of trust in me," she pointed out.

"If I'm going to ask you to trust me, I have to be prepared to trust you."

"That's true."

"What about the girl who's waiting for me?"

"Aliciana?" Rosarita shook her head. "Don't worry about her. She's not very bright, but she's very loyal. She'll do and say whatever I tell her."

The Kid smiled a little. "Then tell her that I'm sorry I won't be enjoying her company tonight. She needs to stay in that room and maybe make some noise every now and then, as if I'm in there with her."

"She can do that," Rosarita said with a nod. "You realize that this is going to cost you, don't you?"

"Of course." He took a twenty-dollar gold piece from his pocket and handed it to her. "If that's not enough, we can discuss it when I get back."

"And if you . . . don't get back?"

"Well, you and Aliciana have made some money, anyway."

"All right." She slipped the coin in a pocket of her gown. "Part of me says you're loco, and an even bigger part says *I'm* loco for going along with you . . . but we'll do what you want. Go down to the end of the hall and turn right into the alcove you'll find there. There are some stairs leading down to a door that opens into the alley behind the building. It's dark back there, and if you don't have a light, no one will see you leaving."

The Kid nodded. "That's just what I need. Much obliged."

"Don't thank me. You're going off to do something that might get you killed, I think, and I'm helping you to do it." She shook her head and muttered, "Loco."

"You'll tell Aliciana what she's supposed to do?"

Rosarita waved a hand. "Go. I'll take care of it."

The Kid nodded and went to the door. He opened it enough to see that the hall was deserted before he pulled it wider and slipped out.

The stairs were where Rosarita said they were, and they were shrouded so thickly with shadow that The Kid had to put a hand on one wall of the stairwell to help guide him as he descended. When he reached the bottom, he found the unlocked door and stole out into the night.

Next was the matter of finding a horse. He couldn't get his own mount from the livery stable without alerting the proprietor, and since he already had to trust Rosarita and Aliciana, he didn't want to involve anyone else in the plan. The more people who knew about something, the harder it was to keep it quiet.

There were plenty of horses tied at the hitch rails along the street, and since he was already a fugitive, he didn't think stealing a horse would add all that much to his troubles. Besides, he intended to bring it back. The animal's owner might not even miss it.

The Kid followed the alley for a couple blocks, then catfooted along the side of a building until he reached the street. After checking carefully to make sure no one was close by, he stepped out, went to the nearest hitch rail, and picked out one of the horses tied there.

He jerked on the reins, swung up into the saddle, and turned the animal. With his hat pulled low to shield his face, he rode unhurriedly out of Gehenna.

Nobody yelled, "Stop! Horse thief!" behind him, and The Kid was profoundly grateful for that.

Once he was clear of the settlement, he urged the horse to a faster pace. There was enough light from the stars for him to spot the landmarks he had noticed on his way into town the night before, so he was able to head in a fairly straight line toward the camp where he had left Carl Drake and Jillian Fletcher.

His heart slugged a little harder in his chest as he thought about them. He would be glad to reach the camp and make sure they were all right.

It took him less than half an hour to get to the ridge where the three of them had reined in the day before and seen Gehenna sprawled in the distance across the Arizona landscape. His eyes searched the night for the clump of trees that marked the campsite. Spotting the trees, he rode toward them at a steady lope.

When he was close, he reined the stolen horse back to a walk and called softly, "Hello, the camp!" He didn't want to ride in, spook Drake, and have the man start shooting at him.

There was no response.

"Drake!" The Kid called. "Jillian! It's me, Morgan!"

Nothing.

Snakes of worry began to slither around in The Kid's belly. He rode closer, moving faster again. The reins were in his left hand. With his right, he drew the Colt.

He rode into the trees, wondering briefly if he had somehow come to the wrong place.

But no, there was the clearing where they'd made camp, and even in the dim light, he was able to make out some of their gear scattered around.

But there was no sign of Drake or Jillian.

They were gone.

Chapter 32

With a feeling of alarm growing inside him, The Kid scouted up and down the area along the base of the ridge. He called out the names of Drake and Jillian, but no one answered.

The Kid turned the stolen mount and rode back to the camp. All five of the horses that had been there when he left were missing as well.

He swung down from the saddle and reached in his pocket for a match, intending to strike a light. His fingers froze on the lucifer as he realized that might be exactly what somebody was waiting for him to do. It was possible a bushwhacker was watching the camp at that very moment. If he lit the match, he would just be giving them a target to aim at.

He hunkered on his heels instead and let his eyes adjust to the darkness as much as they would. After a few moments, he was able to make out scuff marks in the dirt where it looked like there had been a struggle.

Someone had slipped up on the camp, jumped Drake and Jillian, and taken them prisoner. One man couldn't have done that by himself. There must have been at least two of them, possibly even more.

Instantly, The Kid thought about J.P. Malone and Clyde Woods and the way they had been gone from Gehenna for most of the day.

Malone and Woods could have ridden out there and taken some of Bledsoe's other hired gunmen with them. In the short time The Kid had been in Gehenna, he hadn't met all of the gang, so he wouldn't have missed some of them if they were gone.

But why would they have done that, The Kid asked himself. How could they have known that Drake and Jillian were even there?

The Kid couldn't answer those questions. What was important was that his two partners were gone, and he had to get back to Gehenna before his ruse to get out of town without being noticed was discovered. With his face set in grim lines, The Kid mounted up and rode back toward the settlement.

The man who owned the horse might have realized that it was gone, so The Kid decided it would be better not to ride openly into town, as he had ridden out. He circled instead, so he could approach Gehenna without being seen. He would tie the horse behind one of the buildings, where it would be found and returned to its owner sooner or later.

As he rode closer, he didn't hear anything going on except the normal raucous music and laughter. There was no hue and cry, as there would be if the whole town was looking for a horse thief.

He dismounted and led the horse on foot the last couple hundred yards. Reaching a darkened building, probably some business that was closed down for the night, he tied the reins to a post and patted the horse's shoulder. "Thanks for the ride," The Kid whispered. Then he headed up the alley for the back door of Rosarita's place.

No one had come along and locked it while he was gone, he found as he tried the knob a few minutes later. The door opened silently on well-oiled hinges.

He probably wasn't the first hombre to sneak in and out the back door of this whorehouse, he reflected with a wry smile as he started up the stairs, feeling his way along in the shadows.

He reached the top and stepped out of the alcove into the dimly lit corridor. He went to the room where Aliciana was supposed to be waiting for him and eased the door open.

A candle burned in a holder on a small table next to the wall. Its flickering yellow light revealed a shape under the pulled-up sheet on the bed.

For a split second, The Kid had a bad feeling, a premonition of something about to happen that he wasn't going to like.

What if Aliciana was under that sheet with her throat cut? What if Bledsoe had found out somehow who he was and why he was there, and he had taken revenge on the soiled dove for helping him?

Then a soft snore came from the figure on the bed, and with a sigh, The Kid relaxed.

He moved to the bed and sat down gently beside her. She stirred and rolled over toward him, and when he put a hand on her shoulder, her eyes opened and she smiled up at him, looking lovely with her thick black hair tousled around her face from sleep.

"Querida!" she exclaimed. "You came back to me."

"Didn't Rosarita tell you that I would?"

Aliciana shrugged her shoulders, which made the sheet fall away from them and reveal that they were bare. Chances were, she didn't have anything on under the sheet.

"She said you were a *loco hombre* doing things that might get you killed." She slid her arms from under the sheet and reached for him. "I'm glad you didn't get killed."

"The night's not over yet," The Kid reminded her.

She pouted. "Don' talk like that. Now that you're here, we can do wha' we came up here for, eh?"

The Kid took hold of her wrists as she tried to caress him intimately. "As far as anybody knows, that's what we've been doing for the past hour and a half. I need to get back downstairs. I'll bet Dakota Pete is waiting for me."

"Maybe, maybe not. But you paid for all this time. You got to get something out of it."

"I have," The Kid said, although in truth the

only thing he had gotten out of his visit to the camp was a lot of worry.

He had intended to talk to Drake and Jillian and figure out their next move. Now that option had been taken out of his hands. In all likelihood, the two of them were somewhere in Gehenna, since it was the only settlement in the area.

He had to find them. And the first step in that, he had a hunch, would be to find Malone and Woods.

"Now get dressed," he told Aliciana as he patted her sheet-covered hip. "We'll go downstairs together, like we've both been up here the whole time."

With a disgusted snort, she threw the sheet back, confirming his hunch about what she was wearing underneath it—nothing.

"Loco hombre is right," she muttered as she sat up and swung sleek legs out of bed.

The Kid stood up and turned his back while she got dressed. That didn't take long, since it just consisted of pulling the thin shift over her head and then running her fingers through her hair to straighten it.

"You might try to look satisfied," he said as he opened the door and they started out of the room.

"It won' be easy," she said, "but I'll try."

They went along the hall toward the stairs. The Kid thought about stopping at Rosarita's room and knocking on the door to let her know that he was back, but decided it wasn't necessary. Aliciana could tell her later.

"You know not to mention this to anybody but your boss," he told her under his breath.

"Sí, sí, I understand. For what you paid, you get to keep your big secret."

"Gracias," he said as they reached the top of the stairs.

One of the other soiled doves, accompanied by a client, was headed up to her room. They were about halfway up the stairs. The Kid touched Aliciana's arm and stepped back, intending for them to give the couple room to pass.

The Kid wasn't paying much attention to the other whore or the man with her. The man was just a big hombre in a long coat and a wide-brimmed hat. But then he lifted his head to look up at the top of the stairs.

The Kid felt a shock go through him as he recognized the face of Tom Haggarty, the bounty hunter who had shot him, pistol-whipped him, and dragged him to Hell Gate Prison.

That wasn't the worst of it. With widening eyes, Haggarty recognized him, too, and swept the long coat back to claw at the butt of the holstered Colt on his hip.

Chapter 33

The Kid could have outdrawn Haggarty, but Aliciana was right beside him and the other soiled dove was on the stairs next to the bounty hunter. There was too great a chance one of the women might get hit if shots were traded.

Instead of going for his gun, The Kid launched himself down the stairs. Pushing off with his foot, he leaped halfway to the spot where Haggarty stood, flew through the air, and tackled the man. With a yell, Haggarty went over backwards as The Kid hit him from above.

The two of them tumbled wildly out of control down the stairs while the startled whores began to scream.

When they came to a stop at the bottom of the staircase, The Kid was on the bottom and Haggarty was on top. Haggarty's hat had come off during the fall. His thick black hair hung down over his forehead.

Heaving his body from the floor, The Kid shot

his right fist up and into Haggarty's jaw, throwing Haggarty to the side. Momentarily stunned, he rolled across the rug.

The Kid scrambled up, trying to seize the advantage, but Haggarty recovered quickly and made it to his knees. The Kid swung another punch, but Haggarty grabbed his arm and hauled him up and over. The Kid came down hard on his back and found himself lying in the doorway between the foyer and the parlor.

Dakota Pete was sitting in the parlor with the girl he had taken upstairs earlier in the evening. He bolted up from the divan and his eyes widened in surprise as he looked at The Kid lying there on the rug in front of him.

"What the hell?" he rumbled.

The Kid didn't have time to explain. Haggarty was up again. One of the bounty hunter's boots started toward The Kid's head in a vicious kick.

The Kid jerked his head aside just in time and grabbed Haggarty's leg, shoving upward on it, trying to upset the man. Haggarty fell backwards hopping on one foot but managed to stay upright as he stumbled against the foyer wall, hitting it so hard a framed picture crashed to the floor.

The Kid surged up and darted across the foyer. He hammered two fast punches into Haggarty's midsection. Haggarty swung a roundhouse left. The Kid twisted so the blow didn't take his head off, but Haggarty's fist landed on his shoulder and knocked him back. The Kid staggered into the parlor, tripping on a rug. He started to fall again.

Dakota Pete was there to catch him. Pete's hands went under The Kid's arms and held him up. "Kid, what the hell's goin' on here? Who's that varmint?"

Haggarty had recovered enough to reach for his gun again.

The Kid didn't want to kill the man over a case of mistaken identity, but he wasn't going to stand there and let Haggarty shoot him. The Kid's gun flickered out as he still leaned against Dakota Pete. He cleared leather well ahead of Haggarty, and flame spouted from the Colt's muzzle as The Kid fired from the hip.

Haggarty's right arm jerked as the bullet burned across it and thudded into the wall. He howled in pain as his fingers opened involuntarily and he dropped his gun.

It was one hell of a shot, The Kid knew, and probably as much luck as anything else. He had been trying to drill Haggarty's arm, but creasing it like that was almost as good.

He pulled away from Pete and extended his arm, leveling the gun at Haggarty. "Don't move," he told the bounty hunter.

Haggarty didn't listen. He grabbed a small, round, spindle-legged table sitting in the foyer and slung it as hard as he could at The Kid.

Haggarty followed the table with a charge as The Kid ducked away from the flying table. He heard a thud and a grunt of pain as the table struck Pete instead.

The next instant, Haggarty barreled into him. The Kid went over backward. Haggarty landed on top of him, and the brawny bounty hunter's weight drove the breath from The Kid's lungs, leaving him gasping for air.

Haggarty grabbed the wrist of The Kid's gun hand and slammed it down against the floor. The Colt slipped out of his fingers and went spinning away.

The Kid jabbed a punch at Haggarty's face with his other hand. His fist caught Haggarty just above the right eye and opened up a cut. Blood welled from it and dripped on The Kid.

The injury didn't slow Haggarty down. He dug a knee into The Kid's belly and hammered a punch to his jaw. Skyrockets burst behind The Kid's eyes. For a second, it was all he could do to hang on to consciousness.

Suddenly, Haggarty's weight was gone. No longer pinned to the floor, The Kid rolled onto his side and dragged air into his lungs. The blackness that had threatened to envelop him began to recede.

When he looked up, he saw Haggarty and Dakota Pete swaying and stumbling around the parlor as they wrestled and pummeled each other. They were roughly the same size, and The Kid was reminded of the epic battle between Pete and the blacksmith that morning.

Pete had lost that battle, but he appeared to be

winning the one with Haggarty. Slugging furiously, Pete drove the man back.

Then Haggarty caught a break when Pete slipped a little and dropped his guard. The opening lasted only a second, but it was long enough for Haggarty to shoot a piledriver punch through it.

The bounty hunter's fist landed with devastating force. For a second, Dakota Pete's feet left the floor. He landed on a table, splintering it underneath him.

The Kid tried to get up, but his muscles wouldn't work yet after he'd almost passed out. Haggarty wheeled toward him, and it was obvious from the expression on the bounty hunter's blood-streaked face that he intended to kick and stomp The Kid into submission.

With a huge crash of shattering glass, something broke over the back of Haggarty's head. Haggarty grunted, stumbled forward a step, and then fell on his face. Judging from the way he sprawled, he was out cold.

Rosarita stood behind the spot where he had been. She clutched what was left of a big glass bowl in her hands.

"I was just trying to distract him," she said. "I didn't think it would knock him out."

The Kid sat up. "He must have . . . a soft spot on the back of his head . . . like some men have a glass jaw."

Dakota Pete pushed himself into a sitting position and shook his head like a bull buffalo.

He asked thickly, "Wha . . . what in blazes happened?"

"Haggarty knocked both of us down and nearly out," The Kid said. "And then Rosarita knocked *him* out."

Pete's eyes widened in amazement. "She did?"

"I'm as surprised as you are," Rosarita said dryly. "Don't you think you should do something about him before he comes to?"

"Yeah," The Kid said. He made it to his feet and went over to Haggarty. "Do you have any rope, and something we can use to gag him?"

Rosarita called over her shoulder, "Brady! Fetch some rope and a couple of rags. Make it fast."

Pete struggled upright. "Who is that varmint?" he asked. "How come you and him started in with the fisticuffs, Kid?"

"His name is Haggarty. He's a bounty hunter."

The Kid said that as if it explained everything, and to an outlaw like Dakota Pete, it probably did. Pete would assume that Haggarty had recognized The Kid from some wanted poster and tried to capture him.

The Kid didn't want Haggarty spilling the truth and calling him Bledsoe. It was entirely possible that Pete and the other hired gunmen didn't know that Matthew Harrison was really the escaped convict Ben Bledsoe, but The Kid didn't want to take that chance. Better to get him tied up and gagged before he regained consciousness.

They barely managed that. Brady hurried in

with some rope and a pair of rags to use as a gag. The Kid told Pete and the bouncer to tie Haggarty's hands and feet securely, while he worked on the gag. He wadded up one of the rags, shoved it into the bounty hunter's mouth, and tied it in place with the other rag.

Haggarty wouldn't be able to do anything except make some noise, which he did as he began to stir. His eyelids fluttered open, and when he looked up and saw The Kid, angry croaking sounds—curses—came from him.

By then, Pete and Brady had his arms and legs bound so tightly that he couldn't even writhe around.

"What're we gonna do with him?" Brady asked.

The Kid looked at Rosarita. "I hate to have to ask you—"

"Then don't," she snapped. "I already saved your bacon by knocking him out. What else do you want?"

"If you could see your way clear to stashing him here for a while, I'd be much obliged."

Rosarita frowned. "That's what I was afraid you were going to say. For how long?"

"Well, I don't really know. A few hours? Maybe overnight?"

Pete suggested, "It'd be easier just to cut his throat and dump him in the desert for the buzzards and the coyotes."

The noises Haggarty was making got even louder.

The Kid shook his head. "We're not going to

do that," he declared. "But I can't have him running loose around town, either."

Rosarita sighed. "All right, there's an empty room upstairs. If you can carry him up there, you can leave him in it for a while, I suppose. Will someone need to stand guard over him?"

"That would be better," The Kid said.

"Brady can sit outside the door with a shotgun. Will that do it?"

The Kid nodded. "Like I said, I'm much obliged."

Pete said, "All right, gimme a hand, Brady. I reckon between the two of us, we can wrestle him up the stairs." He glanced at The Kid. "I still say it'd be easier—"

The Kid shook his head again.

Pete heaved a sigh and said, "All right, Brady, come on. Let's get this varmint upstairs."

While they were wrestling Haggarty up the stairs, with plenty of accompanying grunts, groans, and curses, Rosarita came over to The Kid and said, "I heard you tell your friend that man is a bounty hunter. I assume that means you're a wanted man."

The Kid didn't confirm or deny that. He just said, "Did you really think I wasn't?"

"Does him showing up here have anything to do with . . . that other matter you were involved in tonight?"

The Kid knew she was referring to the ruse that had allowed him to slip out of Gehenna undetected. He shook his head. "No, I can honestly say that I never expected to see Haggarty again."

"Is him showing up like this going to complicate . . . whatever it is you're doing?"

"It might. It's one more thing to take into account, anyway."

"You need to be careful, Mr. Morgan. If you give Harrison the slightest provocation, he'll have you killed . . . or kill you himself."

"I don't doubt that for a second. I intend to stay alive, though."

"So did everyone else who's crossed him since he came to Gehenna. By helping you the way I have tonight, not once but twice, I've backed your play. If anything happens to you, and if Harrison finds out what I've done . . ."

Her voice trailed off, but she didn't have to finish the sentence. They both knew what she meant. If that happened, she would be left twisting in the wind, and no doubt Bledsoe would have his revenge.

She reached out and squeezed The Kid's arm for a second. "Just don't get yourself killed," she said huskily.

"I'll do my best," The Kid promised.

The problem that had brought him hurrying back to the settlement was still as urgent as ever. He had to find out what had happened to Carl Drake and Jillian Fletcher.

The Kid retrieved his gun and holstered it as Pete came clumping back down the stairs.

"We got the fella locked up in that empty room,"

Pete reported. "Brady's parked hisself right outside the door with a Greener."

The Kid nodded. "Good." He looked around at the wrecked furniture in the parlor and told Rosarita, "I'm sorry about all the damage."

"It's all right," she said. "If there's anything I know about, it's how to collect what a man owes me. Mister . . . Haggarty, was that it? . . . will be paying me back."

As The Kid and Pete left the house, the big man said, "Whew! What a night, eh, Kid?"

"You don't know the half of it."

Pete's elbow nudged into The Kid's side. "You was in that room with that Aliciana gal for a long time. Reckon you must've turned her ever' which way but loose. Or was it the other way around? Haw, haw!"

"I got my money's worth," The Kid said honestly.

"Yeah, me, too. That little gal o' mine was a real spitfire, if you know what I mean. I don't know which one of us got wore out first. It was just about a dead heat."

The Kid didn't pay much attention as Pete prattled on about his amorous achievements. He was trying to figure out what had happened to Drake and Jillian, and his mind kept coming back to the fact that J.P. Malone and Clyde Woods had been gone most of the day.

Maybe Bledsoe, with the natural caution of a wanted man, had sent them out to scour the countryside around Gehenna, just to make sure no one else had shown up along with the stranger known as Kid Morgan. Most people wouldn't think to do something like that, but clearly Bledsoe wasn't a run-of-the-mill owlhoot. He was smarter and more careful than that.

The worry grew as The Kid approached Bledsoe's saloon headquarters. The hour was late, but even so, the place was surprisingly quiet as he and Pete went up the steps to the boardwalk. The player piano had fallen silent, and there wasn't the usual hubbub from the customers.

As he pushed through the batwings with Pete close behind him, The Kid saw the customers were all gone. The big man wasn't trying to block his escape route, but that's what it amounted to.

The place was empty except for five people. Bledsoe sat at his usual table, while Malone and Woods flanked it, standing on either side with their guns drawn.

Two more people sat at the table.

Carl Drake and Jillian Fletcher.

"Come on in, Kid," Bledsoe invited with a cold smile on his face. "I think we have a lot to talk about."

Chapter 34

"What's goin' on, boss?" Pete boomed from right behind The Kid. "Who're those folks?"

The Kid's gaze darted from side to side around the room. The wheels of his brain turned over furiously. He couldn't hope to outdraw Malone and Woods since their guns were already drawn and pointed at Drake and Jillian. If he tried anything, they could blast the two prisoners at point-blank range.

Drake's face was bruised and bloody. They had beaten him . . . and worse. He cradled his left arm and hand against his body. Several fingers were bent at unnatural angles, showing that they had been broken. The tips of the other fingers were crimson ruins where the nails had been yanked out.

They had tortured Drake, and judging by the smug smile on Bledsoe's face, Drake had spilled his guts.

The Kid glanced over his shoulder. Dakota Pete's tall, broad-shouldered body filled the doorway. The Kid might have been able to take him by surprise and get past him, but that would mean abandoning Drake and Jillian to whatever fate Bledsoe had in mind for them.

He couldn't do that.

Instead, The Kid gave Bledsoe a cool, level look and asked, "What is it you want, Bledsoe?"

"Who's Bledsoe?" Pete asked before the boss outlaw could say anything.

"He is," The Kid replied with a nod toward the man sitting at the table. "Matthew Harrison isn't his real name. He's actually Bloody Ben Bledsoe, an outlaw who escaped from Hell Gate Prison in New Mexico Territory a couple months ago."

Bledsoe laughed. "You're not telling anyone here anything they didn't already know, Morgan, except for Dakota, of course. J.P. and Clyde weren't aware of it until tonight, when we . . . convinced . . . Carl here to start talking, but it doesn't really matter. And of course the lovely Miss Fletcher already knew. We remember each other from Hell Gate, don't we, my dear?"

Jillian didn't say anything. She looked pale and frightened, but also defiant.

"I'm sorry, Kid," Drake rasped out as he hunched over his mutilated hand. "I held out . . . as long as I could . . . but I had to tell 'em . . . how you and I busted out together and came after him."

Pete shook his head and said, "I sure ain't followin' what's goin' on here."

"You don't have to," Bledsoe snapped. "Just don't let Morgan get past you."

"Sure, boss. But he don't look like he's tryin' to go anywhere."

"You sent Woods and Malone out to have a look around, didn't you?" The Kid asked, putting into words the theory he'd been turning over in his mind a few minutes earlier, before everything had gone to hell. "You didn't trust me?"

"Why the hell should I?" Bledsoe demanded. "You show up out of the blue, kill my best gunman, and take his place. It sounded like something a damned U.S. marshal or some other lawman would do. I sent the boys out to make sure there wasn't some posse waiting outside of town for you to give them a signal." Bledsoe smirked. "Instead they found these two. That's a pretty sorry posse, Morgan. Of course, as it turns out, you're not a lawman. Just another outlaw."

The Kid shook his head. "No. A man who wants to clear his name."

He didn't say "an innocent man." That term would never really apply to him again. Not after some of the things he had seen . . . and done.

Bledsoe nodded and said, "Yes, Drake and Miss Fletcher told us about how some bounty hunter caught you and dragged you to Hell Gate, thinking that you were me. To tell you the truth, I don't see that much resemblance, myself, but obviously other people do. You fooled that bastard warden." Bledsoe looked over at Drake. "But you knew right away that he wasn't me, didn't you, Carl?"

"Yeah," Drake husked. "I did."

"But you figured he could help you find me and even the score for me double-crossing you, right?"

"Yeah." Drake looked at Bledsoe with hate burning in his eyes. "It occurred to me. And that's the way it worked out."

"Until you reached the end game. That's a chess term, although you probably don't know that. I outmaneuvered you, Carl, and you've lost. You won't be getting what you came after." Bledsoe turned to look toward the door. "Dakota, take Morgan's gun."

Pete hesitated. "Boss, I'm still all mixed up. But The Kid and me, we've sorta become friends. I'd hate to see anything bad happen to him."

Bledsoe sat forward and frowned. "You've only known him for a day, you big lummox! Now do what you're told."

Pete sighed and reached for The Kid. "Sorry," he muttered.

The Kid knew if he lost his gun, he and Drake and Jillian were all done for. He had to act, no matter how risky it was.

He twisted and grabbed Pete's arm as the big man reached for him. With a grunt of effort, he heaved Pete around so that the thick body partially shielded him from Malone and Woods. His hand flashed to his gun. The Colt leaped up and flamed as he fired under Pete's arm.

The bullet grazed Malone, sending him backwards. At the same time, The Kid gave Pete a hard shove that sent him stumbling toward Woods.

The gambler held his fire and darted to the side, trying to get an angle on The Kid.

He was already moving, throwing himself backward through the batwings. He didn't want to leave Drake and Jillian behind, but he had no choice. He stood a lot better chance of helping them if he was free than if he was Bledsoe's prisoner.

Guns roared. Bullets punched holes through the batwings and chewed splinters from the swinging doors.

But The Kid was already gone, racing down the boardwalk, then leaping around the corner of the building. He had to stay on the move. Bledsoe had a lot more men besides Malone and Woods working for him. Within minutes, they would be searching the town for him, no doubt with orders to kill him on sight.

The odds were overwhelming against him . . . but he might have an ally that Bledsoe didn't know about. It was a long shot, but he had to try.

He headed for Rosarita's.

The back door was still unlocked. Gun drawn, he went up the stairs and looked around the corner from the alcove at the top. Brady sat dozing in a chair leaned against the wall, a shotgun across his lap.

"Brady!" The Kid called softly as he approached.

The chair's front legs thumped against the floor as the bouncer opened his eyes and sat up. He started to lift the scattergun in alarm, but The Kid already had hold of the barrels and held it down.

"Take it easy, Brady, it's just me, Morgan."

Brady blinked bleary eyes at him. "Oh. Yeah. I

see that now. You come back for that fella we got locked up inside?"

"I have to talk to him, yes," The Kid said with a nod.

Brady stood up and took a key from his pocket. "Lemme get the door."

As Brady was unlocking the door, the door of Rosarita's room opened and she peered out into the hall. "What's going on here?" she asked as she clutched a dressing gown at her throat. "Kid, is that you back here already?"

"Yeah."

A worried frown appeared on Rosarita's face. "I heard a shot a little while ago. You had something to do with that, didn't you?"

"Yeah, I'm afraid so. I have to talk to Haggarty."

"The bounty hunter? Why?"

A humorless grin pulled at The Kid's mouth. "I'm going to give him a chance to get his hands on the man he's really been after all along." The Kid stepped past the fat bouncer and saw the trussed-up Haggarty lying on the floor of the room. Haggarty made angry noises through the gag and thumped his bound feet against the floor.

The Kid holstered his gun and kneeled beside the man. "Listen to me, Haggarty," he said. "If you won't yell, I'll take that gag out of your mouth. We need to talk."

Haggarty glared at him but fell silent.

"I'll take that as a yes," The Kid said. He started untying the rag that held the gag in the bounty hunter's mouth.

When it was loose, Haggarty spat out the gag. He worked his jaw around for a minute before saying hoarsely, "You son of a bitch, Bledsoe."

The situation was too dire for The Kid to feel exasperated at being called Bledsoe again. He said, "Shut up and listen. For the last time, *I'm not Ben Bledsoe.* But the real Bledsoe is right here in Gehenna, so if you want him, you've got a chance to get him."

"You don't expect me to believe—"

"I expect you to believe your own eyes. And besides that, Jillian Fletcher is here, and so is Carl Drake. They both know the truth."

"Miss Fletcher's still alive?"

"Of course she is."

"Well, that's one mark in your favor, I guess," Haggarty said. "When I heard that you'd taken her hostage when you and Drake broke out, I figured you'd kill her somewhere along the way. I started to hope she was still alive when I didn't find her body anywhere along the trail."

"You followed us all the way from Hell Gate?" The Kid asked.

Haggarty nodded. "Yeah. I was in the area when I heard about you escaping with Drake. I was able to pick up your trail. I've been dogging it ever since. When I came to this whorehouse tonight, I figured on asking some questions, finding out if anybody had seen you." He grunted. "I never expected to run right into you while I was going up the stairs."

"Well, here's the deal, Haggarty. You and I are going to have to work together."

"Work together? To do what?"

"Like I told you, the real Bledsoe is here in Gehenna. He's holding Drake and Miss Fletcher prisoner."

Quickly, The Kid explained how Bledsoe had come there and taken over his old hometown after escaping from Hell Gate and picking up the loot he had hidden before his capture.

"Even having to pay those gunmen, he's probably got a bigger stash now," The Kid went on. "He's been bleeding this town dry."

"If he's surrounded by hired killers, he won't be easy to take," Haggarty commented.

The Kid chuckled. "You believe me now, do you?"

"It's too loco a story to make up." Haggarty's eyes cut over toward the door. "Anyway, they seem to believe you. Maybe you're telling the truth."

The Kid glanced in that direction and saw Rosarita and Brady standing there. They had been listening to his story.

Brady said, "I've been around these parts for a long time. I remember that old drunk, Silas Bledsoe. Seems like he had some shiftless kid, but I'm not real clear on that."

"That boy grew up to be Matthew Harrison?" Rosarita asked.

"Before that, he was Bloody Ben Bledsoe, and before that, he was Professor Bledsoe," The Kid said.

"Quite a life," Haggarty muttered. "It doesn't change anything, though. He's still a no-good outlaw with a price on his head."

"Yeah. If I cut you loose, you'll help me take him and free Drake and Miss Fletcher?"

"Drake's going back to prison, too," Haggarty snapped. "He's a murderer and a thief."

The Kid shrugged. "He probably belongs behind bars, all right. I won't stop you from taking him. So what do you say, Haggarty? I have your word that we'll work together?"

Haggarty drew in a deep breath and nodded. "My word," he said. "I'm going to give you a chance to prove that you're telling the truth. But if you're not, if this is some sort of trick, then God help you. And even if it's not . . . the odds are mighty high against us. We may wind up getting killed."

"I know," The Kid said. "Brady, fetch a knife so we can cut these ropes. Haggarty and I have work to do."

"Not by yourself," Brady said. "I'll back your play, too, Morgan."

The Kid looked at him in surprise. "You will?"

"Damn right. I know it's only been a few weeks, but I'm sick and tired of Harrison or Bledsoe or whatever the hell his name is lordin' over the whole town."

"So am I," Rosarita said. "Everyone in Gehenna is. My girls and I can't really help you fight him, Kid, but there are men in town who would."

"Like the blacksmith," Brady suggested. "And the fella who owns the livery stable."

"And a dozen more," Rosarita said. "I could send my girls out to find them and talk to them, tell them to meet here with their guns."

"They'd be risking their lives," The Kid warned.

"Letting Harrison run things is just a slower way of dying."

The Kid thought it over quickly. Raising a force of townspeople to storm the saloon would go a long way toward evening the odds. There was a good chance some of them would die.

But people had been fighting for their freedom and dying even before the country was born, he reminded himself.

"All right," he said. "But Bledsoe will have men out looking for me. Your girls will have to be careful not to be seen, and so will the men who gather here, or Bledsoe will know that something's up."

Rosarita nodded. "I understand. Brady, cut Mr. Haggarty loose. I'll wake the girls and tell them they have some work to do." She smiled. "Different work."

Brady took a clasp knife from his pocket and began sawing through the bonds around Haggarty's wrists. "Gonna be a lot of changes in Gehenna tonight," he said.

"Because of fighting Bledsoe, you mean?" The Kid asked.

"Yeah, that . . . and the way a bunch of soiled doves are gonna be showin' up at the houses of some of the town's leadin' citizens asking them for help. Some fellas are gonna be doin' a lot of explainin' to their wives in the mornin' . . . if they live through the night!"

Chapter 35

The Kid was a little wary when he gave Haggarty his gun back, but the bounty hunter appeared to be keeping his word. He holstered the weapon and asked, "What's the plan?"

"Once the rest of the men get here, they're going down to the saloon to confront Bledsoe," The Kid explained. He looked at the bouncer. "You'll be in charge of them, Brady."

"Me?" the fat man asked in surprise. "I'm no gunfighter."

"No, but you're a citizen of this town, and you'll present it like you're taking the town back from Bledsoe."

"A challenge like that will just get us all killed!"

The Kid shook his head. "No, you'll all find some good cover before you ever call out to Bledsoe. Some of you need to aim at the saloon, while the rest of the bunch gets ready for Bledsoe's men who are scattered through the town to come running when the shooting starts."

Brady rubbed his heavy jaw as he frowned in thought. "You mean they'll come runnin' right into an ambush."

"That's right," The Kid said with a nod. "They'll be out in the open and ought to be easy pickings while the rest of you keep Bledsoe and his men who are in the saloon pinned down there."

"Well . . . it might work," Brady admitted. "Those sons o' bitches will put up a fight, though."

The Kid nodded again. "Of course they will. That's why I said this would be dangerous. But if you want your town back, you'll have to fight for it."

"I reckon that's true." Brady's voice strengthened as he went on, "We'll do it. But what are you gonna be doin', Kid?"

The Kid inclined his head toward the bounty hunter. "Haggarty and I are going to get into the saloon and take Bledsoe by surprise."

"We are?" Haggarty said.

"That's right. I expect you're anxious to see him with your own eyes, so you'll know that I'm telling the truth."

Haggarty's burly shoulders rose and fell. "I wouldn't mind."

"He has Miss Fletcher and Drake in there. I figure when all hell breaks loose outside would be a good time to go in and get them."

Haggarty thought it over and then nodded. "All right. Sounds like a good idea. I want Bledsoe alive, though."

"We'll try. I can't make any promises."

A savage grin tugged at Haggarty's mouth. "I could always take you back again, you know. Fletcher believed it once."

"He won't again. Not after talking to his daughter."

"Yeah, you're probably right. All right, we'll do the best we can to take him alive and leave it at that."

The Kid nodded in agreement. He turned back to Brady.

"Haggarty and I are going to slip out the back and get in position. We'll wait until we hear the shooting start to make our move."

"You don't reckon there's any chance Harrison— Bledsoe, whatever the hell his name is—will give up when I yell out and tell him to get out of town, do you?" Brady asked.

The Kid didn't answer that.

Brady sighed. "Yeah, that's what I thought." He held out his hand. "Good luck, Kid."

The Kid shook hands with the bouncer. Rosarita hugged him, whispering in his ear, "The invitation is still open, Kid, any time. Just come back alive."

He embraced her but didn't make any promises.

The Kid and Haggarty slipped out the back door of the whorehouse, disappearing into the thick shadows in the alley. Even though The Kid had been in Gehenna only a little more than twenty-four hours, he knew the town better than the bounty hunter did, so he took the lead.

They had gone only a few yards when a figure suddenly loomed out of the darkness in front of them. The Kid knew instantly it had to be one of Bledsoe's hired guns searching for him, even before the man asked in a whiskey-roughened voice, "Who—"

He didn't get any further than that. The Kid whipped out his gun, but not to fire. They couldn't afford a gunshot right now.

Instead he twirled the gun so that when he struck with the speed of an uncoiling diamond-back rattler, it was the butt that crashed into the man's head. He went down like a sack of stones. The only sound was the thud of the gun butt against his skull and the fainter thud of his body hitting the ground in the alley.

"You get him, Kid?" Haggarty whispered.

"Yeah." The Kid knelt and used his fingers to explore the depression in the man's head. Shattered bone moved under his fingers. The hired killer wouldn't be waking up.

The Kid straightened and breathed, "Let's go."

The two men set off again for the saloon.

They didn't encounter any more of Bledsoe's gun-wolves along the way. The Kid recognized the building that housed the saloon when they came to it, but he wasn't familiar with the rear of the place. Working by feel, he found a door, but it was locked.

"I can probably bust it down when the time comes," Haggarty said into The Kid's ear, so quietly that no one could have heard the words a yard away.

"Yeah, but if you couldn't, that might ruin everything. Anyway, it would warn them that we're coming."

"You got a better idea?" Haggarty asked.

The Kid looked up and spotted a window on the second floor that was open a few inches. "Yeah," he said as he pointed it out to Haggarty.

"How do we get up there?"

That was a tougher question to answer. The Kid started looking around the alley.

He found an empty crate. He thought if Haggarty were to stand on the crate, and he climbed up onto the bounty hunter's shoulders, he would be able to reach the windowsill and pull himself up. Then maybe he could give Haggarty a hand somehow.

"I suppose we can give it a try," Haggarty agreed. "Just don't make any racket."

They put the crate in place. The big question now was whether it would support the weight of both of them. Haggarty was a big man, and The Kid, though slender, wasn't exactly a lightweight.

All they could do was try. Haggarty climbed onto the crate and flattened his hands against the wall to brace himself.

The Kid stepped up onto the crate and started climbing the bigger man. It was awkward and uncomfortable, and he almost slipped a time or two.

But he finally managed to get a foot on Haggarty's shoulder and hoisted himself up. He leaned against the wall with one hand and reached up as high as he could with the other.

His fingers closed over the sill.

The Kid hung on tightly and got his other hand on the sill. Below him, Haggarty grabbed his ankles and lifted him even more. The Kid hooked one arm over the sill and used the other hand to push the window up more. He hoped it wouldn't squeal too loudly as it opened.

It made some noise, but not much. The room within was dark, but that didn't mean it was unoccupied. Somebody might well be waiting in there right now to kill whoever was sneaking in.

He levered the upper half of his body up and over the sill, then rolled the rest of the way into the room.

Nothing happened. The room was quiet.

The Kid got to his feet and stuck his head out the window to nod to Haggarty. He turned back into the room and felt around until he found an empty bed. Pulling the sheet off, he began tearing it into strips that he quickly knotted together to form a makeshift rope.

After tying the rope to the bed, he wrapped it around his waist, then dropped the rest of it out the window. He felt Haggarty take hold of it. The Kid sat down and braced his feet against the wall under the window as Haggarty's weight made the rope cut into him.

The Kid kept his teeth clamped together so he didn't make any sound. Haggarty felt like he weighed a ton, and it seemed like it took him an hour to climb up to the window, rather than a minute or so.

At last Haggarty pulled himself through the window and sprawled on the floor next to The Kid.

"Made it," he said, and the gasp in his voice indicated that the climb hadn't been easy for him.

The Kid unwound the rope from his body, grateful the wide leather gunbelt had kept it from cutting too deeply into his flesh. He got to his feet, as did Haggarty.

"What now?" the bounty hunter whispered.

"We wait for Brady and the men with him to make their move," The Kid replied.

They didn't have long to wait. Even though the open window was on the back of the building, they heard Brady's shout from the street a few minutes later.

"Harrison! Hey, Harrison, you hear me?"

The Kid eased open the door. It led onto the balcony that overlooked the saloon's main room. A hubbub of surprised voices drifted up from below.

A moment later, Bledsoe's voice called, "Who's out there? Speak up, damn you!"

"It's the whole town," Brady shouted, "come to tell you to take your gunmen and get the hell out!"

"Kill that fool," Bledsoe snapped.

The Kid hoped Brady had sense enough to duck for cover.

A second later, shots roared down below and were answered by a thunderous volley from outside. It sounded like a small-scale war had broken out in Gehenna, which was about what it amounted to.

The Kid looked at Haggarty and nodded.

Both men drew their guns and stepped out onto the balcony.

Chapter 36

The scene spread out before them wasn't unexpected. Several of Bledsoe's gunmen were crouched at the saloon's front windows, which had been shattered by the gunfire from outside. They were returning the fire as fast as they could.

Back in the corner, Jillian and Drake still sat at the table with Bledsoe, while Malone, Woods, and Dakota Pete stood tensely nearby with guns in their hands. The three gun-wolves were going to protect their boss.

Bledsoe's eyes caught the movement as The Kid and Haggarty stepped out. His head jerked up and he stared at them in shock.

He wasn't the only one who was surprised. Haggarty had time to mutter, "Son of a bitch! I wouldn't have believed it if I didn't see it with my own eyes!"

Then Bledsoe surged to his feet as his hand clawed under his coat for a gun. He shouted, "On the balcony! Kill them!"

With the speed and instincts of true professional killers, Malone and Woods whipped their revolvers up and opened fire. Flame was already spouting from the muzzles of the Colts in the hands of the two men on the balcony.

Shots thundered in the saloon. Splinters flew from the railing along the front of the balcony as slugs struck it. The Kid felt more than heard the wind-rip of bullets past his ears.

He didn't panic. His cool-nerved steadiness allowed him to put two bullets in J.P. Malone's chest. Malone dropped his gun and went over backward as crimson welled from the wounds.

Beside The Kid, Haggarty's gun roared and bucked as well, and Clyde Woods doubled over as the steel-jacketed rounds punched into his guts, shredding them. He collapsed face-first on the table in front of a horrified Jillian.

Bledsoe had his gun out, but before he could fire, Dakota Pete bellowed, "No!" and struck with his own pistol. The barrel thudded against Bledsoe's skull and dropped the boss outlaw senseless on the floor beside the table.

Pete let go of his gun. It fell on the table. He thrust both hands up to shoulder height and shouted, "Hold your fire! Don't shoot, Kid!"

The sudden outburst of violence inside the saloon had taken the gunmen at the windows by surprise. One of them jerked up to his feet and had started to turn when a rifle cracked somewhere outside and drilled him.

As that man flopped to the floor, Brady bounded

in through the batwings carrying a shotgun. He swung the Greener at the second man and fired just as the man got a shot off. The slug tore through Brady's leg and knocked him off his feet, but the load of buckshot had done a lot more damage to the gunman, blasting him out through the broken window in a bloody heap.

That left just one gunman. The blacksmith, Bonham, who had rushed into the saloon right behind Brady, took care of him with a swing of the big hammer in his hand. The killer went down with his skull crushed by the blow.

A few more shots sounded outside, but the battle in the saloon was over.

The Kid straightened from the gunfighting crouch into which he had instinctively dropped as he traded shots with Malone. He looked down at the big Viking standing with his hands up and asked, "Are you out of this, Pete?"

"Damn right I'm out of it," Pete rumbled. "I never did cotton to some of the things Harrison had us doin'. Robbin' banks and holdin' up trains is one thing. Stealin' from ordinary folks and killin' 'em if they stand up to you is another."

"All right. Move away from the table." Gun in hand, The Kid started down the stairs trailed by Haggarty. "Bonham, see if you can tie up that wound in Brady's leg." The Kid hurried over to the table. "Miss Fletcher, are you all right?"

She looked pale and shaken, but as far as The Kid tell, she wasn't wounded. She confirmed that by nodding and saying, "I'm fine, Kid." She summoned up a weak smile. "You were supposed to call me Jillian, remember?"

The Kid chuckled, although it sounded out of place in the room choked by acrid clouds of gunsmoke that were only slowly drifting away.

"How about you, Drake?"

The man nodded. "Yeah, except for what that bastard did to me earlier." He spat on the unconscious Bledsoe.

"There's probably a doctor in town," The Kid said. "We'll have him take a look at your hand and see what he can do for you."

A couple of townsmen carrying rifles stepped in from the boardwalk. "Is it all over in here?" one of them asked.

"Yeah," Brady replied as Bonham tied a rag around his bloody thigh. "What about out there?"

The man nodded. "We got 'em all, except for a couple who grabbed horses and lit a shuck when they realized they'd run into an ambush."

The Kid knew that two fleeing hardcases wouldn't cause any trouble. The men probably wouldn't stop running until they were a long way from Gehenna.

Haggarty loomed over Bledsoe's unconscious form. He shook his head.

"It's still hard to believe, but that's him, all right. We'll tie him up and find a secure place to keep him until we're ready to head back."

"Who the hell are you?" Drake asked.

"Name's Haggarty," the bounty hunter said. "I'm taking you and Bledsoe back to Hell Gate, Drake."

Drake looked over at The Kid. "Morgan?"

"Sorry, Drake. I appreciate your help, but it's out of my hands. I made a deal with Haggarty."

"You made a deal with me, too, damn it."

"And I kept it," The Kid snapped. "We found Bledsoe. I couldn't do anything about how things played out after that."

Haggarty nodded toward Dakota Pete. "How about this big fella?"

"You have any paper on him?" The Kid asked.

Haggarty thought about it and then shook his head. "No, not that I recall."

"Then you don't have any claim on him."

Haggarty shrugged. "That's fine. I've got Bledsoe and Drake. That'll be a nice payoff."

Supported by the blacksmith, Brady limped over to the table. "You need us for anything else, Morgan?"

"No, I don't suppose so."

"Good. We got a town to clean up, now that it belongs to its real owners again."

An hour later, The Kid stood on the boardwalk in front of the saloon and looked up and down Gehenna's single street. Everything looked quiet and peaceful. The bodies of the dead gunmen had been hauled to the undertaker's, along with the two townsmen who had been fatally shot in the battle. The wounded had been tended to by the harried town doctor. Bledsoe and Drake were locked in a windowless storeroom at the back of the saloon, and Dakota Pete stood guard outside the door. Haggarty clearly didn't like not trying to collect a bounty on Pete as well, but for the time being, they had become allies.

A soft footstep behind The Kid made him turn. His hand started toward his gun, but he relaxed as he recognized Jillian Fletcher.

She moved up beside him. "It's hard to believe this is all over," she said. She stood close to The Kid, close enough that he could feel the warmth of her body. "There's a part of me that doesn't want to go back to Hell Gate."

"I know what you mean. I'd just as soon never see the place again." The Kid smiled in the darkness. "But I am looking forward to the look on your father's face when he sees me and Bledsoe and realizes he was wrong."

"Don't expect him to apologize. I know he's my father, but . . . he's not a very good man, I think."

The Kid didn't say anything. Whatever Jillian believed about Fletcher, she would have to come to terms with it on her own.

She went on, "I hope that on the way back, you and I can . . . get to know each other better."

Both Rosarita and Aliciana had expressed similar sentiments a short time earlier when The Kid paid a visit to the whorehouse to make sure everything was all right there. He had turned them down as gently as possible, and he intended to do the same with Jillian. It was still too soon for him to get involved with another woman, whether it was just for their mutual, momentary pleasure, or something more.

When the time was right, if it ever was, he would know it.

For the time being, he gave Jillian a non-committal, "We'll see," then went on, "You'd better go on over to the hotel and get some sleep. It's been a long day and a longer night."

"Yes, I know. It seems almost like a waste, since it'll be light in a couple of hours—"

The sound of another footstep stopped her. Both of them turned to see that a man had come up behind them. The Kid tensed as a rifle came up in the man's hands.

"Jillian, get away from him!" Jonas Fletcher ordered. *"Now!"*

Chapter 37

"Father!" Jillian gasped.

She wasn't any more surprised than The Kid was. As far as he had known, Fletcher was still in New Mexico Territory, at Hell Gate Prison.

Obviously, that wasn't the case. The man was right there, pointing a rifle at him, and The Kid knew that the whole mess wasn't over at all.

In fact, it was about to get worse.

"Get away from him, Jillian," Fletcher said again.

"Father, wait," she pleaded. "This isn't Ben Bledsoe. He was telling you the truth before. His name is really Kid Morgan."

That wasn't completely true, but it was close enough.

"I know he's not Bledsoe, damn it," Fletcher grated. "I've known that ever since about a week after Haggarty brought him in."

That revelation sent a surge of anger through The Kid. "You knew?" he asked in a low, dangerous voice. "You knew I wasn't Bledsoe, but you pretended you thought I was and put me through all that hell anyway?"

"I had to make your situation dire enough that you'd have no choice but to take Drake up on his offer and break out," Fletcher said with a smirk on his face.

Understanding broke in The Kid's brain with stunning force. "You and Drake are partners!"

"That's right. He and Bledsoe were supposed to break out together, and Drake would leave a trail I could follow while Bledsoe led him to that fortune in stolen loot he had hidden. But then Bledsoe double-crossed Drake by escaping without him, after I'd set up the whole thing to make it easy for him."

"Is Drake even a real convict?"

"Oh, yes," Fletcher replied. "A cold-blooded killer who double-crossed his own men. That brute Otto was right about him, you know. But Bledsoe proved to be even more devious. I sent my men after him, but he gave them the slip. I was about to give up on ever getting my hands on that money . . . and then you dropped right into my lap."

"Father, I . . . I don't believe any of this," Jillian said, sounding shaken.

"Believe it," he snapped. "You think it's been easy sitting there watching your mother dying, knowing that if we were rich, there might be something I could do to help her?" Fletcher gave a shake of his head. "Well, it doesn't matter now," he said with brutal harshness. "She died right before I left Hell Gate to follow you and Morgan and Drake."

Jillian put her hands over her face. Soft but terrible sobs came from her.

The Kid was certain Fletcher hadn't come all that way by himself. He would have brought men with him, possibly some of the guards from the prison but more likely hired guns, since his goal was to steal the money Bloody Ben Bledsoe had already stolen. If Fletcher wasn't as big an outlaw as Bledsoe was, it wasn't for lack of trying.

"I can't believe you'd risk your own daughter's life like that," The Kid said contemptuously. He wanted to keep Fletcher talking until he found out as much as he could about the danger facing him.

"That was Drake's idea, not mine," Fletcher said. "I told you, the man has a penchant for treachery. Jillian was never supposed to be involved, and it was just an accident that she was. Since she's here, though, she can help me." His voice sharpened. "Jillian, stop that crying and take his gun."

"Wha . . . what?" she asked as she lowered her hands.

"Take Morgan's gun, or I'll just go ahead and kill him." He sounded disdainful as he added, "A few moments ago you sounded like you have feelings for this drifter, although I don't see why. If you don't want him dead, do as I say."

She turned her head to look up at The Kid.

"I . . . I'm sorry," she said as she reached out with both hands to lift his Colt from its holster.

"That's all right," The Kid said. "I reckon this has thrown you for a loop, too."

"Where are Bledsoe and Drake?" Fletcher asked as Jillian stepped away from The Kid.

"What are you going to do with them?"

"Make Bledsoe tell me where to find that money, of course. And kill Drake."

"You'll be the fugitive then, Fletcher. You'll never be able to go back to Hell Gate."

"There's nothing there to go back to," Fletcher said bleakly.

Since the crooked warden had the drop on him and Jillian was still close by, in the line of fire, there was nothing The Kid could do except say, "They're locked up in a storeroom in the back of this saloon."

"Fine. Let's go."

Jillian said, "Father, you have to promise that you won't hurt Mr. Morgan or anybody else."

"Of course, of course," Fletcher said. "I just want the money."

The Kid didn't believe him for a second. Fletcher didn't intend to leave any witnesses alive behind him—which meant that Jillian would be forced to spend the rest of her life on the run with him.

The Kid hoped she realized that. He turned and pushed through the batwings into the saloon. Fletcher was right behind him, accompanied by three hard-faced gunmen he motioned out of the shadows of the alley beside the building. Jillian, looking dazed, brought up the rear, still holding The Kid's revolver.

The Kid opened a door leading into a short hallway. At the other end of the corridor was the storeroom where Bledsoe and Drake were locked up. Dakota Pete sat in a ladderback chair in front of that door.

Pete looked up in surprise when he saw The Kid, and surprise turned to alarm when he spotted Fletcher and the three gunmen. He said, "Kid, what the hell?" as he came up out of the chair. His hand moved toward his gun.

"Take it easy," The Kid said quickly. "They've got the drop on us, Pete. And they want Bledsoe and Drake. Get the two of them out here."

Pete frowned. "Kid, are you sure?"

"I'm sure." The Kid hoped that while Fletcher and the other men were distracted by Bledsoe and Drake, he and Pete would be able to make a move. The prospect of getting their hands on a lot of loot was too much for most men to ignore.

Pete turned the key in the lock. Fletcher ordered, "All right, come away from there. Get out into the main room."

His men covered The Kid and Dakota Pete. Meanwhile Fletcher approached the door of the storeroom and called, "Bledsoe! Drake! It's all right. Come on out."

The door opened. Drake emerged first, followed by Bledsoe. Both men looked wary, but an expression of relief washed over Drake's face as he recognized the warden.

"Fletcher!" he exclaimed. "I thought that was your voice, but I wasn't sure. Thank God you got here. We're going to clean up. Bledsoe's got even more than we thought—"

"That's good to know," Fletcher said. He brought the rifle to his shoulder and fired.

At that range, the slug smashed into Drake's chest and knocked him back against Bledsoe, who caught him and kept him from falling. Blood bubbled from the bullet hole and a crimson trail wormed its way out of Drake's mouth. His eyes were wide with shock and disbelief.

"That's for double-crossing me and putting my daughter in danger," Fletcher said. "And one less share of the loot, of course."

Drake's eyes glazed over in death. Bledsoe let go of him, and he crumpled.

"Come on out, Bledsoe," Fletcher ordered.

"Sure, warden," Bledsoe said with a faint smile on his face. He emerged from the hallway into the big main room of the saloon. "It's good to see you again. From the way you were just talking about a payoff, I'm assuming that you turned out to be as big a crook as I am, is that right?"

"Shut up," Fletcher snapped. "Where's the loot?"

"What's left of it is in the safe in my office," Bledsoe answered easily. "Plus three or four times as much that I've collected here in Gehenna. It's all yours if you let me go. Better yet, stay here. We'll be partners. I need some good men on my side. We'll finish taking this town for all its worth."

Fletcher blinked rapidly as he frowned. "Partners?" he repeated. "You and me?"

"Why not?" Bledsoe asked. "We're both intelligent men. Working together, we can make a fortune here, and when Gehenna is bled dry, we'll move on and do it again somewhere else."

The barrel of the rifle in Fletcher's hands lowered slightly. "I never thought about that," he mused. "It might work out quite well—"

"No!"

The strangled cry came from Jillian. The Kid turned to look at her and saw that she had lifted his revolver in both hands and was pointing it at her father as she backed away.

"Jillian, what in blazes are you doing?" Fletcher snapped. "Put that gun down right now."

Jillian shook her head. "No," she said. "No, this has gone on long enough. I . . . I just watched you murder a man in cold blood, Father!"

"Carl Drake barely qualified as a man," Fletcher said dismissively. "He was an outlaw."

"Like you!" Jillian accused.

Fletcher shook his head impatiently. "Stop this nonsense right now. If you don't put that gun down, one of my men will take it away from you."

He made a curt gesture, and one of the hardcases took a step toward Jillian. It was just a feint, though. As she jerked the gun toward him, another man moved to grab her from behind.

Jillian realized what was about to happen and twisted back toward her father, pulling the trigger as she did so. She cried out as the gun roared and the recoil tore it from her hands.

Fletcher staggered back and stared down in shock at the blood on his side where the bullet Jillian had fired had creased him.

The Kid moved at the same time, diving and reaching out to catch the gun Jillian had dropped before it hit the floor. As soon as the walnut grips slapped into his palm, he rolled over and came up on a knee.

Fletcher swung the rifle toward him. Flame gouted from the muzzle. The bullet plowed into the floorboards beside The Kid as the Colt began to roar. The Kid slammed three shots into Fletcher's chest in little more than the blink of an eye.

Meanwhile, Dakota Pete took advantage of the distraction to grab one of Fletcher's men and lift the hardcase off the floor. With a bellow of rage, Pete swung the man like a club and sent him crashing into the other two gunmen. All of them sprawled on the floor.

They still held their guns, and as The Kid lunged up and darted to the side, slugs whipped past him. He returned the fire, and so did Pete, the shots pounding out like deafening drumbeats.

As the echoes died away, The Kid saw all three of the hired guns lying there bullet-riddled, bleeding their lives out.

That left Bledsoe.

Another shot blasted suddenly. The Kid heard the bullet sizzle past him. He turned, saw Tom Haggarty standing in the doorway, one hand holding the batwings open while the other clutched a revolver with smoke curling from the barrel.

The Kid looked in the other direction in time to see Ben Bledsoe fold up. The rifle he had picked up after Fletcher dropped it slipped from his fingers as he fell to the floor and gasped a couple times before a spasm went through him. After that, he lay still.

"I heard the shots and figured I'd better see what was going on," Haggarty said as he lowered his gun. "Looks like I got here just in time."

The Kid nodded his thanks. "Just in time to save my life, from the looks of it. I'm obliged, Haggarty."

The bounty hunter smiled thinly. "The reward notices on Bledsoe *did* say dead or alive. I can take his body to Tucson and collect that way."

The sound of sobbing made The Kid look around again. Jillian knelt beside her father's corpse. She appeared to be unhurt, but her face was wet with tears when she looked up at The Kid and said, "I . . . I shot him. My own father."

"You didn't kill him," The Kid told her. "I did. And if you want to hate me for that, I don't blame you."

"H-hate you?" Jillian repeated. "No. No, I can't do that. The man you killed . . . he wasn't the man he . . . he used to be. The one I . . ."

She couldn't go on. She collapsed across Fletcher's body, her back shaking with sobs.

Conrad Browning had suffered his own tragedies and hadn't been able to deal with them. That was why Kid Morgan had been born. He sure as hell couldn't make the pain and the conflicting emotions go away for Jillian Fletcher.

So The Kid did the only thing he could.

He punched the empties out of his Colt's cylinder and thumbed in fresh rounds to take their place.

The sun came up an hour later. By midday, Tom Haggarty had already left Gehenna, driving a wagon with the blanket-wrapped bodies of Ben Bledsoe and Carl Drake in the back of it. The owner of the local wagonyard was letting him use it to take the bodies to Tucson out of gratitude for the part Haggarty had played in freeing the settlement from Bledsoe's iron-fisted grip.

"You don't have to worry about being a fugitive anymore, Morgan," Haggarty had told The Kid before he left. "I'll make sure the authorities over in New Mexico know it was a case of mistaken identity."

"I'm obliged for that." The Kid had said.

"One more thing . . . I brought along that buckskin of yours that I took when I left you at Hell Gate. He's over in the livery stable. Wherever you're going next, you'll need a horse."

The Kid was grateful for that, as well, and as he lifted a hand in farewell while Haggarty drove away, he wondered if he would ever see the bounty hunter again. Haggarty wasn't a bad sort . . .

For a tough, mean son of a bitch.

The Kid had the buckskin saddled up, and he had a packhorse loaded with supplies ready to travel, too, courtesy of the merchants of Gehenna, who were glad to have their businesses back. Both animals were tied to the hitch rail in front of the hotel.

As The Kid started up the steps to the porch, Jillian came out of the front door and waited for him. The tears on her face had dried, but she still looked grave.

"You're leaving so soon?" she asked.

"There's nothing to keep me here," The Kid said.

"There could be." She glanced down the street toward Rosarita's place, where Rosarita herself stood out front with Aliciana and several more of the soiled doves. "In fact, I think you could take your pick of reasons."

The Kid smiled and shook his head. "I'd be lying if I said I wasn't tempted . . . but I think I'll be riding on."

"Just you and whatever pain it is that you're carrying inside you?"

"Something like that," he said. "What about you? Are you going back to Hell Gate?"

"Why would I? There's nothing for me there. I was thinking I might stay here in Gehenna. It seems like a nice town, even though it has a terrible name."

"Names can be changed," Kid Morgan said.

"Yes, but does that really make any difference in what a place is, or who a person is?"

"We can hope," he said with a shrug. He put a hand on her shoulder, leaned closer to brush a kiss across her forehead, and turned back to his horses. "So long, Jillian," he said over his shoulder.

She didn't say anything else, or smile, or wave, but he felt her watching him as he rode away.

Dakota Pete walked out from the blacksmith shop as The Kid rode by. He said, "I wish you'd stick around for a while, Kid. Bonham's gonna teach me blacksmithin'. I figure it's time I had a trade besides law-breakin'."

"That's probably a good idea," The Kid said with a smile. "I don't think you're really cut out to be an outlaw, Pete."

"Where are you headin'?"

"That's a good question. Maybe I'll figure it out when I get there."

Pete called, "So long!" as The Kid rode away. The Kid turned in the saddle and lifted a hand in farewell.

Would he recognize his destination when he finally found it, if he ever did? Or was he doomed to wander endlessly, a solitary rider, a loner in search of the peace he might not ever find?

The Kid didn't know. The only way to find out was to keep riding.